Amish Sisters Marry

Abigail's Admirer

Book 3

By Rose Doss

ISBN: 978-1-955945-51-6

Cover images courtesy of dreamstime
Interior image from Brandi Lea designs
Cover by Joleene Naylor.

Manufactured/Produced in the United States

CHAPTER ONE

"You're making a complete mess of the backyard!" Abby angrily yelled at the blond giant standing in front of her.

Eli Probst scooped his broad hat off the ground, using his forearm to swipe at the sweat on his forehead as he grinned at her. "Drilling does make a mess."

The *Mann* standing in front of her was tall and muscled and she hated that she'd even noticed this.

He also was naked from the waist up.

Abby swallowed and glared at him. She really hated that she had a hard time ripping her gaze from his highly-muscled nakedness.

The early Ohio summer sun shone down on her head and bees buzzed in the lavender bushes that circled the kitchen garden and she reminded herself that she'd seen before a *Mann* without a shirt. She had brothers. She'd been married, for heaven's sake.

"You've made a mess in the yard!"

The blond giant looked around at the piles of dirt, the mud pits in the yard and trampled grass everywhere.

"We have to do that to drill the well for you," he said in a cheerful voice.

"This is horrible. Does *Daed* know about this? Holes filled with water! Dirt piles everywhere. What is that big tower thing? Can't you do it without making this huge mess?" She braced her fists on her hips.

"No," he answered, seeming to find her ire funny.

This just made Abby madder.

"They're big holes and dirt piles! These are enough! And the grass is all muddy. I hope you plan to put everything back the way you found it," she snapped, convinced this wasn't possible.

"I'll do my best after we put up the windmill." Eli smiled, brushing aside a bee that droned against his broad arm.

He didn't seem the least bit concerned that he might get stung...or that she was yelling at him. In fact, she didn't think much would upset him.

"And what is all this pipe and stuff in the yard?"

"Didn't your *Daed* tell you? We're going to build a windmill to pump the well water into a storage tank that will be—." He turned to gesture toward the deepest yard area, beyond the barn. "—back there."

His cheerfulness annoyed her—and she knew this didn't make sense.

While she was glad that they'd no longer have to hand pump water to carry into the Haus, the size of this business appalled her. "How long will all of that take?"

"Several weeks. A month or so," he responded with unimpaired cheerfulness. "Kinda depends on what we run into. Rocks. Boulders. I could be in your back yard for a while."

"Months!" The thought was dismaying...and that upset her more than anything. Seeing Eli Probst every day for that long!

Abby shuddered.

Abigail Eichelberger needed to get unstuck, she thought later that afternoon.

She saw now that she had to create a new life for herself. Abe had been dead now for three years and she still lived in her parents' home. She just wasn't sure how to move on. Maybe she should drive out with the Bishop.

The five sisters were lounging in Abby, Naomi and Faith's room, the supper stew still cooking on the stove.

"I think," her sister, Becca, said as if she'd heard Abby's thought, "that Bishop Bechtel would make you a good husband."

"No!" Dinah, Abby's just-younger sister, exclaimed. "The bishop is forty-five years old, if he's a day, and he has five children."

Abby grimaced at her. "I'm twenty-eight now myself—not a spring chicken--and, as I'm not likely to produce *Kinder* for him, Bishop Bechtel having children is a good thing."

"Don't be ridiculous," Dinah objected. "You and Abe were only married five years. You can't conclude that you'll never conceive."

Dinah had just gotten engaged to the *Mann* who employed her in his kick scooter shop and they were to be married after the harvest that fall, not that this was generally known. It wasn't *Gott's* wish that they be proud of marriages—or births, although they were all excited that Becca was with child.

Naomi, their next-to-the-youngest sister, said in a practical tone, "All the younger *Menner* who've come around are of no interest to you. You might need to widen the pool."

She was munching on an apple, having ensconced herself on the window seat. "Don't look at me that way, Dinah. I'm just saying what Abby herself has said."

Raising her eyebrows with a quirk of her mouth, Abby made a confirming gesture. "I did."

"Bishop Bechtel isn't her only choice. I think Abby needs to use a matchmaker," Faith declared brightly.

Her words brought a wave of protests.

"How can you say that?" Dinah objected.

As the youngest of the sisters, at fifteen Faith generally had to make big declarative statements to be heard. "There's nothing wrong with using a matchmaker! We know several marriages around here were made that way. Not everyone wants to marry a neighbor."

"Or a cousin," Becca said gloomily from her place on the bed. "Nothing but trouble doing that."

Abigail reflected that it still seemed strange to see Becca's rounded shape. Of the sisters, Abby had been the first to marry. She should have had the first grandchild, but in the five years of her marriage to Abe she hadn't produced any offspring.

"I still say she can find a husband here," Becca said stubbornly. "Bishop Bechtel may not be attractive to any of you, but he might fit Abby's needs."

Laughing, Abigail waved a hand. "I think we shouldn't worry about my needs. Becca, when did the midwife say you're due?"

The next afternoon, Abby stood in the kitchen, looking out the window in the back door at several sedge wrens and dickcissels in a tall red oak in the backyard. Behind her, Abigail's younger sisters, along with their grandmother and mother, were canning snap beans. The room was buzzing with the women's chatter.

Grossmammi Ruth sat at the table with *Mamm*, snapping the beans while her two sisters cleaned the glass jars they'd use.

"Here," Naomi directed Faith. "Check every jar for chips and cracks around the neck. We don't want anything to keep them from sealing."

Over her shoulder, Abigail asked, "Does the stove need more wood?"

"I don't think so—"

Abby heard Naomi's voice suddenly from a distance, her gaze falling from the oak tree to the men preparing to drill in the back yard.

A tall tower was cinched down to the ground to apparently keep it from moving. From what she could see, all three *Menner* on Eli's crew were there, including himself.

The tall, blond head of the crew again wore no coat, but he did have a shirt, this time. He'd rolled up his shirt sleeves, however, and even at this distance, Abigail could see the hair on his arms.

She swallowed.

4

Watching, Abigail saw Eli Probst lift above his head a rod of several feet and drive it into the ground. One of his helpers lifted a beam of some sort attached to the tower and then the other helper pulled it down while Eli again lifted and drove it into the ground.

They'd clearly done this before and Abigail couldn't care less. It was mildly interesting, but her gaze kept returning to the sight of Eli Probst's broad, muscled back and powerful arms. He was really a sight, driving the rod deep into the hole they were making.

"Abby, Abby?" Naomi's voice intruded into her thoughts. "Are we ready?"

With a deep sigh that she didn't want to examine, Abigail turned away from the window.

"The service was fine. I thought the Bishop's message was important," *Mamm* said the next Sunday, having come from the kitchen to join the rest of the family at the tables outside. She raised her face to the sun. "It's a lovely day."

"It is," Abigail agreed, preferring to talk about the weather rather than anything about the Bishop.

"*Mamm*," Faith piped up, "don't you think Abby should consider using a matchmaker?"

"I think," their *Daed* said in his deep voice, "that we should finish our lunch and not dwell on others' business."

Zach Cassel, the young *Mann* from the farm next to theirs, walked down the row of tables outside the *Haus*. "Zook *familye*! This is fine June weather we're having, isn't it?"

"So, lovely!" *Mamm* agreed. "I thought I saw your *Mamm* earlier, Zach, but I can't find her now."

"*Neh*, she left," Zach said with a shrug. "My *Schweschder's* new *Boppli* has kept Eve up most the night. *Mamm* went to care for the baby while my sister sleeps."

"Of course." *Mamm* nodded in sympathy. "*Bopplin* can be difficult to get to sleep."

Abigail didn't say anything, reflecting that dwelling on her own lack of *Kinder* wouldn't help anyone. She was barren and she had to just accept that fact.

"I don't see Naomi," Zach said, looking along the table.

"She's still helping in the kitchen," Dinah said. "She's doing clean up this week."

"Ahhh. Well, tell her I said *hallo*." With a wave, the Cassel boy loped off.

"Is Levi still here?" Abigail asked.

After she'd cried when hearing Levi make a remark about Abe having died childless, Dinah was overly-sensitive about having fallen for Levi. Abigail was careful to demonstrate her acceptance of him.

He'd apologized to Abigail, assuring her that he hadn't known she was within earshot.

Abby knew, too, that he'd lost his own wife and newborn not long before making the comment. No one knew better than Abigail the toll that kind of loss took on a person. She was determined, though, that she needed to move on with her life.

It was important that Dinah see the two had resolved their conflict.

Abigail's challenge was that she hadn't found anyone who she enjoyed as much as Abe, no *Mann* that she could see herself taking as a husband. *Gott* had told them to marry and produce children. She couldn't seem to do the second and she hadn't been inspired to marry again. Even letting other *Menner* take her hand left Abby cold. Certainly, this wasn't the way it should be.

Perhaps, she should let the Bishop move forward in his courtship and simply accept matters as they were between them. At least, she could care for his children and give them a loving home.

Abigail stared into space, trying to envision that path. She could definitely care for his *Kinder*, but sleeping next to the Bishop was another thing.

Dear Gott, she prayed, *help me with this. Shall I accept the Bishop as my husband? Please help me know how to move my life forward. I know there is a reason why I didn't die in that accident with Abe? How do I now best follow your word?*

"I'm glad you came," Eli told his father the next day. "Does the drilling setup seem good to you?"

Behind them in the Zook backyard, Thomas Meili, one of Eli's two helpers, coiled the rope they used to pull up the pipe before thrusting it in to dig the well. His other helper—James Schmidt—was still unloading the work buggy.

The drilling set up was very good. Eli knew this as he'd been his *Daed's* site foreman for several years, but it was good to have his father's approval of the job.

Although June weather was progressing fine, a scud of clouds had settled over this afternoon. Eli stood in the Zook backyard next to Jobe Probst with a damp, gray light filtering through the beech, elm and oak tree branches overhead.

"It looks fine," Jobe said in a grudging voice.

Eli didn't say anything in response to this. He knew that it was difficult for his father to let him take over the business. *Daed* probably didn't know what to do with himself.

Jobe walked around the drilling rig, eyeing it from different sides. "You could have added a fourth leg to the rig."

"I know, but remember that we've done the three-legged rig for the last year or so and it's worked fine." He'd work in the business with his *Daed* since he was a *Youngie*.

"I know, I know," his father said in the same grudging voice.

"The job is going well and we have another one lined up here locally for July. I can move straight from this one to that."

"Your mother and I are worried that you need to settle down!" his *Daed* blurted out, frowning fiercely at Eli. "It's all well and good that you're attending to the jobs, but when are you ever going to find another wife?"

Eli glanced down at the pile of dark earth turned from the drilling rig.

"I had a wife, *Daed*," he responded in a mild tone at variance to his father's manner. Abigail Zook's beautiful, angry face flashed through his mind's eye. She was a fine woman, even though she wasn't happy about the mess his drilling caused.

He'd been right about her being spicy.

"I know you and Joanna were married," his father returned in an irritable voice. "She's been gone quite some time now. Are you never marrying again? Your *Mamm* and I want grandchildren."

Chuckling, Eli asked, "You mean more than the seven you have?"

"*Yah!*" his father snapped. "More than seven. They are not your children, *der Suh*!"

"No, they are not," agreed Eli. "Father, you and I have worked hard at this business. That has been my focus, not finding a new wife."

"Maybe, but this business cannot build you a home or give you a joyful *familye* to come home to. Perhaps rather than buy Jethro a farm, I should have given the business to him."

As this wasn't the first time his *Daed* had said something similar, Eli remained calm. "Perhaps, but Jethro loves his farm and his life on it."

"Well, then, Adam or Peter."

Eli just looked at his father, saying finally, "I know you and *Mamm* want the best for me."

"We do," his father snapped, his tone at odds with his sentiment.

"I will marry again," Eli promised. "And give you more grandchildren. You just have to let me do this in my own time."

"There are lots of *Maedels* in our town who are eager to marry a *Mann* with a good business."

"I'm sure there are," Eli agreed. "But none of them have seemed like what *Gott* intends for me."

His *Daed* snorted. "*Gott* intends for you to find a *Maedel* and make a home, not for you to make excuses."

CHAPTER TWO

"Becca's certainly beginning to look like she's with child," Dinah remarked the next week.

The Zook sisters all sat around a large quilting frame with their mother, while *Grossmammi* sat in the rocker to the side, nursing a cup of coffee.

"*Yah*, she does," responded *Grossmammi* Ruth with a chuckle.

"I wonder if she'll have a girl or a boy," Faith mused. "Won't it be fun to have a Boppli in the family?"

"It will," *Mamm* said, snapping the thread in her hand in half.

The front door was open to let in the fresh summer air and the *Menner* hadn't returned yet for lunch.

Abigail sat at the quilting frame, dipping her needle into the cotton fabric of the quilt in small, neat stitches. She had nothing to add to the current topic, and so kept quiet. She felt only happiness for Becca, but it was hard not to think of her own empty womb when she saw her sister.

She'd prayed about this many times and now reminded herself that *Gott* knew best. Perhaps she was to nurture another woman's child. The bishop's five children had no living mother and there were others in the same state.

Gott had reassured His people many times that He loved them and that their faith in Him allowed Him to deliver them.

Abigail sighed. She'd just always thought that she'd be delivered with *Kinder* of her own.

"What do you think, Abby?" Faith asked. "A girl or a boy?

Smiling, Abby said, "I'm sure we will love it, either way."

"Of course," Naomi said in her measured voice.

"As the first grandchild in the family, she should call it Adam or Eve." Faith continued stitching, apparently not aware of the shaft that her words sent through Abigail.

She should have been the first to have a baby. Adam hadn't found a wife after his last courtship had fallen apart and he was two years younger than her.

It should have been her, but she needed to move forward from the limbo she'd been in since Abe died.

The time had long since come.

The next Sunday, Abigail paused at the top of the Bassler *Haus* porch steps and looked out over the rolling green hills. She took a deep breath as she stood there before heading down to her buggy after visiting her friend, Grace Bassler.

Hearing male laughter off to the side of the house, Abby turned to see Grace's husband, Rufus Bassler, and Eli Probst coming around from where the Bassler barn was located.

Struck at the unexpected sight of the blond, strapping Eli, she hesitated, all of a sudden, not sure what to do.

"You're *narrish*, Rufus!" Eli said, laughter still in his voice. "I'm not sure we should put the well there without talking to Grace, but there's no problem in doing it, as far as I'm concerned. I can start your well after I finish the Zook well. I'll be at the Zook farm longer than we'd expected—as we hit rock while drilling— but I'll come here next. I still say you should clear the well placement with Grace."

Abigail froze, her body feeling disconnected from her brain. She hesitated there at the top of the steps, not sure what to do. Which was stupid. She knew of no reason not to walk down the porch steps to get in her buggy.

Still walking toward the front of the *Haus* with Eli, Rufus chuckled, his head turned to look at the man who had this stupid effect on Abby.

"I don't think it's crazy to put the well in Grace's kitchen garden. She won't mind. It'll be less distance to carry water to the plants."

"This is between you and your *Frau*," Eli returned with a grin, shaking his head.

Unmoving, her hand on the stair rail, Abigail debated turning to head back into the house. Grace would think it strange of her, since she'd already said her goodbyes, but she'd look no stranger than standing here, as if stricken by the sight of him.

Normally, she didn't feel this unsure of what to do.

Just at that moment, Eli looked up, seeming to have felt her presence.

"*Hallo!*" he called out. "I didn't know you were here. We could have ridden over together from your *Haus*."

"I was visiting Grace," Abby said stupidly, for some reason thinking this needed to be made clear.

Rufus lifted his head to look to where she stood above them on the porch, his gaze uncurious. "Abby! Are you headed home now?"

"*Yah*," she responded as naturally as possible. "I am."

"We can see who gets there first," Eli joked, "although I'm sure that—being from around here—you know all the shortcuts."

She forced her stiff smile to widen. "Probably and I doubt our buggy horses would want us to race."

Why did this Mann make her heart pound?

"Ahhh, my Nellie is a great horse," Eli assured her. "She'd definitely give it her all."

Abigail continued to smile, hoping it didn't look as strained as she felt.

As if it were the most natural thing in the world, Eli extended his hand. "Here. Let me help you into your buggy."

She'd been getting in and out of buggies all her life with no trouble, but she had the urge to take his hand.

Swallowing, Abby made herself continue down the steps with her hand on the rail. Even Abe had never offered that gallantry.

"Let's ask Abigail about the well placement," Rufus suggested. "Abby, do you think Grace would mind having a well in her garden? I think it would be good!"

Having reached the bottom of the steps—glad that Eli had dropped his outstretched hand—she said in a natural voice, "Not if the well digging messes up the things she's already planted, which it will. You should see the mess in our back garden. Trampled grass, mud holes and piles of dirt."

"Digging a well does make a mess," Eli confirmed cheerfully. "Thomas, James and I have to tear up the yard to get the bore down to the water."

"Why *hallo, Frau* Eichelberger," Bishop Bechtel said a smile, standing in front of her in the shade of the tree.

Abby sat with friends at a table in the Lehman yard after the service the following week.

"Hallo," she replied, smiling back pleasantly and giving no hint of her acute understanding of what could transpire between her and the burly, older *Mann.*

"I hope you enjoyed the service," he said, genially.

"I did," she replied, registering again that this was a simple *Mann.* Marriage to him would mean being a *Mamm* to his orphaned children. While that aspect of being the next *Frau* Bechtel didn't bother her at all, she felt no more for the Bishop than kindness toward another human.

Abby knew that shouldn't deter her from accepting his advances, but she'd felt so passionately in love before.

An image of Eli Probst flashed before her mind's eye. He was nothing like Abe, but, Heaven help her, he made her heart beat faster.

"I'm glad you enjoyed the services," he said. "We are having good weather, are we not?"

"Yah, lovely." She kept the smile on her face.

Next to her at the lunch table, Grace Bassler nudged her, interrupting the awkward moment. "I'm sorry, Bishop, but, Abigail, isn't that Eli Probst over there? The *Mann* drilling your well? The one Rufus talked to about drilling one for us?"

Abigail glanced in the direction her friend pointed. "*Yah,* that's Eli."

"I believe he's drilling wells for several in the area," the Bishop said, also looking over. "The farmers here are blessed to have a well driller come this way."

"Yes," Abby said, hating that she felt this flicker inside of her when the muscled blond giant was around. This shouldn't be!

In all the years of widowhood, no other *Mann* had drawn this response from her. Of course, she hadn't had all that many *Menner* show interest in her, probably because she hadn't born children in her marriage. Dinah said the reason more *Menner* hadn't approached the widow Eichelberger was that Abigail sometimes seemed cool and not responsive, but Abby didn't think that would stop a *Mann* who was really interested.

As Eli turned to walk suddenly toward her table under the tree, Abigail looked down at her hands clasped together in her lap.

"*Guten Tag, Frau* Eichelberger," Eli said cheerfully as he approached.

"*Hallo,*" she replied as calmly as she could muster.

"How are you this fine day?"

"I am good."

"Did you make this *gut* lunch?" He patted his flat stomach.

"Yes, I helped," Abigail answered with a smile before it occurred to her that she didn't need to smile at him.

"*Yah,*" Bishop Bechtel chimed in. "Our *Fraus* make the best lunches."

"I was surprised to see you here, Eli," Grace inserted cheerfully in the gap after this statement.

"Oh, yes," he said, "I love visiting every service in the towns where I work. Thomas Meili and James Schmidt, my helpers, often come with me if they don't go home to their families."

"How far from home do you go for work?" Abigail asked, the question popping out of her mouth before she knew it. Generally, she measured words before speaking, so this took her by surprise.

Eli smiled warmly at her. "About a hundred miles in each direction. I could drive home on weekends, but we often work on Saturdays and I get to see my *familye* in between jobs. My *Mamm* and *Daed* understand. This was *Daed's* business. He was away off and on, all my childhood. I took over the business from him."

"Oh," she said. Stretching her mouth into a responsive smile, Abby thought to herself that it was good he'd be moving on soon. She didn't know why this *Mann* made her so awkward.

"Come on, Abby" Faith coaxed, "You might as well play softball with us. You came to the Sing."

Around them, chattering *Youngies* lined up to exit the Lehman *Haus* that evening, excited for the game.

"Everyone isn't playing." Abigail demurred. "*Frau* Luthi and *Frau* Reese are helping *Frau* Lehman in the kitchen to get the desserts ready for after the game."

"Leave her alone," Naomi recommended calmly. "So what if she hides out in the kitchen? At least, Abby came. Let her make small steps."

"I'm not hiding out in the kitchen!" Abigail exclaimed.

"Then, come play," Faith insisted with an encouraging smile. "You are great at softball. Remember, you taught Dinah how to pitch so well."

"I haven't played in years," Abby demurred.

"That doesn't mean you've forgotten how," pointed out the logical Naomi.

"Come on." Faith grabbed Abigail's hand, pulling her toward the door. "I bet both teams will argue over who gets you as pitcher."

"Particularly as Dinah's not here," agreed Naomi, following behind them.

With her new resolution to get unstuck in mind, Abigail let herself be towed to the Lehman front porch, registering the bright afternoon sun and green yard in front of her.

The door behind them opened and banged shut.

"Thank goodness, I finished up in time to get here before the game started," Eli Probst announced cheerfully as he caught up with the three sisters as they descended the porch steps to the yard.

Suddenly, as Abigail felt the hairs on her arm stand up like goose flesh, she took a deep breath and tried to stay calm.

"Abby's going to pitch in the softball game!" Faith announced, still tugging her sister toward the wide area in front of the house.

"I knew there would be a game," he responded with a smile, "but not that *Frau* Eichelberger would play."

"See?" Abigail said, pulling her sister to a stop. "It wouldn't be right for a—a *Frau* to play."

Faith and Eli gave a loud, protesting outcry to this.

"Nothing is said that people who have married cannot play games," Naomi commented. "Remember that the seniors here have a softball game every week."

"Not the women," Abby protested in a low voice. She knew she fell into a very narrow category. Most *Amishe* who were widowed quickly married again and the women were too busy with their family chores to play softball.

"You heard Naomi," Faith tugged her forward again. "Nothing says you can't play."

By this time, Abigail's reluctant feet had brought her right up to the three *Menner* who were making up the teams.

"And you, Jakob, play right outfield for the blue team. Sarah Allebach, you go to second base for the red team," a *Mann* in his twenties directed, making notes on a small tablet. "Dan Otzinger, you're tall. You should play first base, probably for the red team, as we already have a first baseman for the blue team."

Resisting her younger sister's urging to step closer, Abby hung back. She recognized Hiram Neuhaus, the *Mann* assigning players to the two teams. Hiram had been in the same class at school with her and Abe.

He turned toward her just then, his face lighting up when he saw her. "Abby! Are you playing? Tell me you are. The blue team desperately needs a pitcher."

Abigail blinked. She hadn't been expecting this kind of response, particularly since everyone in their *Gmay* knew exactly how long she and Abe had been married and that there had been no *Kinder* born to their union.

"*Yah,* she's here to play," Naomi said, from over Abigail's shoulder.

"Do you want Abby to pitch?" Faith's eagerness was almost palpable.

"I do," Hiram confirmed. "From my memory, you're one of our best. Better even than Dinah, and she's good."

"She is," Naomi agreed, "but she's not here today."

"That's a pity," Hiram commenting, scribbling on his tablet. "Micah would have been glad to give the position up to her."

Abigail could see that he cared more about her softball skills than whether or not she had children.

It was a relief. When her initial grief over Abe's death had subsided some, she'd been hesitant to join her *Geschwischder* at Sings, although all the siblings had once come.

She'd enjoyed playing softball. It felt good being on a team.

To the sides of the make-shift ballfield, the two teams clustered and several <u>Frau</u> sat to the side with their *Kinder.*

She'd not known so many women were in the kitchen. Abigail found herself wishing she didn't have such an audience for her return to pitching.

At that moment, she realized that Eli was on the other softball team, chatting and teasing as if he'd known the other players all his life, instead of only a few weeks.

She firmed her mouth, adjusting the ball glove on her left hand. This part was familiar, but she hadn't played with the *Youngies* since marrying Abe.

It seemed so long ago.

Her teammates took their positions on the bases and in the outfield.

Abby threw the ball to the *Mann* who was playing catcher...and then saw Eli Probst stepping up to the plate, bat in hand.

As he was on the other team, she'd already figured out that she'd be pitching to him, but she hadn't planned on his playing first.

Drawing in a breath, Abigail focused on tossing the ball across the home plate, aiming for the strike zone. She told herself that the *Mann* standing there with a bat was like any other player.

It didn't matter who he was.

She pitched one ball and Eli didn't swing at it. Trying not to register too much about him, she saw that he shuffled his feet in the batter's box and swung the bat several times before cocking it over his shoulder.

Bending forward, she sent another ball over the plate.

Still, he didn't swing.

They both went through their pre-pitch rituals again and Abby felt her nerves tighten. Taking a deep breath, she let another ball fly and then Eli swung. His bat hit the ball with a crack. Abigail swiveled, her glove still on her left hand.

Eli's hit sent the ball in between first and second base. Jakob Ramseyer, playing first base for the red team, ran to scoop up the ball and—acutely aware of Eli pounding toward first base—Abby ran to cover it. She turned to catch the ball that Jakob threw to her.

Turning with the ball in hand to tag Eli out, Abby saw that he was only several feet from where she stood in front of the base and he was thundering toward her.

Bracing herself for the certain impact, Abby was both startled and relieved to feel Eli's hands grab her shoulder and—rather than knock her over—bring her tight against his body.

To her relief, she held onto the ball, but his big, warm body slammed into hers with a force that would have knocked her over if Eli hadn't held her tight against him. Her mouth fell open with the shock of impact and she sucked in a breath of musky man-scent.

The press of his hard body against hers caused reverberations and a wave of heat she couldn't explain. The possibilities were too disturbing.

"Sorry," he said, setting her gently several inches away from him.

The ball still clutched in her glove, Abigail gave him a shaky smile before she gave a jerky nod and walked with trembling legs back to the area occupied by the pitcher.

Not even Abe had this kind of effect on her. It was distressing, particularly since Eli Probst wasn't the sort of *Mann* she saw herself with.

As Abigail waited till the next batter stepped up, she realized she wasn't actually sure she knew the sort of *Mann* she saw herself with.

"Miss Abigail!" Eli exclaimed, finding his arms again full of Abigail Eichelberger as he turned around suddenly. It was the Monday morning just a day after they'd played softball at the Sing. "I'm so sorry."

He'd been pulling a tangled rigging rope in the torn up backyard of the Zook *Haus* and turned around to bump into Abby.

Here they stood in the backyard of her home, Abby clutched up against his chest. He'd drawn her up against his chest just trying to keep from knocking her over.

Even as he registered that his voice had dropped into a husky range, his fogged brain tried to frame his apology.

The sun had risen several hours ago and he'd seen the Zook *Menner* leave to work in the fields as he and Thomas arrived. Not that Thomas or James were here now.

He could think enough to be glad they weren't present at this moment.

His workers had gone into town to get a few supplies that they needed to dig further on the well and they probably wouldn't return for an hour or so.

Abigail's Admirer

The backyard was empty except for he and Abby, none of the other Zook *familye* members having come out of the *Haus* with her.

Oddly, he and Abby seemed frozen in spot despite the warmth of the day, the sun shining down on them, her lithe body still in his arms.

Eli heard the drumming of what had to be his own blood in his head and a bird song from a tall tree nearby.

His mouth felt dry, and all he registered in a fuzzy way was that the woman in his arms was very, very soft.

She licked her lips nervously and Eli felt his head tilt down toward her.

Abby Eichelberger looked so kissable.

Everything seemed to go still around them, the bird even suddenly silent.

As she didn't push him away and seemed to be rising up to meet his kiss, Eli bent even closer to her—

"Abigail!"

The sound of her younger sister calling Abby's name had them both jumping apart.

Now, one of the Zook *Maedels* came outside!

He registered that Abby turned toward the sister and Eli drew in a ragged breath.

"Becca is here to visit," her sister called, walking toward them. She stopped to look between them as if she suddenly felt the air charged as she came further into the garden, even though they'd jumped apart.

"*Hallo*, Mr. Probst."

"*Hallo*," Eli responded, swallowing before he smiled.

"How is the drilling going?" the younger sister asked, cheerfully.

"Very well," he said. "Paused now as my helpers had to go to get more rope."

Eli was very, very glad the girl hadn't walked into the backyard minutes before. He didn't know what was happening between him and Abby Eichelberger, but he liked it.

CHAPTER THREE

"Here, Bishop," Mary Zook said that Sunday afternoon, offering a plate of cookies. "Have another."

The ponderous *Mann* smiled, reaching for another cookie. "I don't mind if I do. You are such a good cook!"

Abigail, sitting on a chair near the sofa, felt her mother's gaze touch her and deliberately widened her smile.

"I've taught everything I know to my *Dochders.*"

"Your girls are very fortunate," the bishop replied. "And their husbands fortunate!"

Mary laughed gaily. "We have one that is married and another soon to be wed, but the others still haven't found the right *Menner*.

Aware that her *Mamm* was being painfully open, Abigail looked down. She knew she needed to find a *familye* and settle down, but need her *Mamm* be so obvious?

"Abel is out, settling the stock in the barn," Mary said at random. "I'm sure he'll be inside in a moment."

Not if Abigail was correct in her father not being thrilled to spend time with the dull Bishop Bechtel.

Not that *Gott* loved him any less. Abby just wasn't sure she wanted to spend the rest of her life with the *Mann.*

"*Hallo*, son!" Abel Zook, the father of the Zook *familye,* greeted the young *Mann* who walked into the backyard several days later.

The early July sun shone down cheerfully on the trampled and muddy yard, which now held several mud pits, connected by a shallow trench.

Eli looked up, momentarily distracted from the drill rod that he was cleaning again, using a bucket of water.

"Eli," Abel said warmly, "this is Levi, my *Dochder*, Dinah's soon to be husband. I know you won't think I'm bragging about this."

"*Hallo*, Levi," Eli offered with a friendly smile, nodding at the bucket of water in front of him. "Forgive me for not offering my hand."

"Of course," Levi responded. "You are clearly working hard. Dinah said that you dig water wells."

"I do," Eli confirmed, "and I'm making a mess of the yard. Thank goodness, I don't need to disturb the kitchen garden!"

All three men laughed.

"Levi," Abel said more seriously, "you and Eli have something in common. You are—well, Eli still is—both widowers. Levi was alone for years."

"That's a club I'd wish on no *Mann*," Levi said, "although I'm very blessed to have finally found my Dinah."

Eli looked at him without expression. "May I be so blessed."

Glancing out the window in *Mamm* and *Daed's* bedroom the next Monday, Abigail was grateful that she'd seen clouds darkening the skies in time to rush to gather the laundry from the line. Rain could now be heard drumming on the roof, drips falling into the bushes outside.

She smoothed a hand over the newly-made bed and gathered up the basket with the sheets she'd replaced, Going into the shadowed hall, she left the basket in the laundry room and pushed open the screen door to the back porch. The sound of the rain was louder and its lovely smell grew stronger.

Abigail didn't immediately notice that the porch was occupied.

"*Hallo.*" Eli smiled from a rocker bench several feet away. "James and Thomas are sheltering from the rain in my buggy, but sitting here on the porch gives me the chance to watch the rain on your yard."

"The messy, torn up yard?" she asked mildly, letting the screen door close behind her.

He laughed. "*Yah.*"

"I think your mud pits will be full of rainwater."

"They certainly will," Eli agreed, "but that's not a problem. The ground will be softer and that'll make tricky footing to push the drill rods the rest of the way down, but I reckon we will find a way."

"And leave even more of a mess from slopping around on the grass," Abigail said, her mouth quirked to one side. She stood in front of the laundry room door, her face lifted as she enjoyed the rain cloaking the porch.

"Probably."

Glancing over, she saw his white teeth in the shadowed light as he smiled in response to her observation.

"It's sad, really, to leave such a mess behind you," Abby observed.

"And clean well water. Don't forget that." Eli patted the bench next to him. "Come sit a while. The rain is lovely to watch."

For a moment, she considered telling him that she was far too busy for his nonsense, but the lure of damp air and the sound of falling rain lured her to stay. At least she told herself that's why she walked over to sit sedately next to him on the bench rocker.

"I love rain," he said simply, "don't you?"

"I do," Abby responded, returning the smile he sent her.

They sat for a few minutes in silence, the only sound of the rain tapping on the roof.

Slowly, Abby felt herself relaxing into the rocker, the beautiful dampness and the quiet presence of the *Mann* beside her lulling her into breathing out in a low sigh.

"I met Dinah's husband," he commented in idle conversation after a moment. "Abel introduced us."

Abby turned her head toward Eli. "Yes?"

"*Yah*. Levi seems like a nice *Mann*."

"He is," she agreed. "We like him very much. More even because he loves Dinah so much."

Eli nodded. "He came to the yard when we were getting ready to continue drilling."

"Levi is very kind." She smiled, thinking of her sister's new husband.

"I can see that and he said he feels blessed to have found Dinah." Eli used his foot against the porch to start the bench rocking.

Nodding, Abby matched his movement.

"Your *Daed* said Levi lost his first wife and that we have this in common."

"He did?" Abby let this new information about Eli sink in. "You lost your first wife?"

"*Yah*," Eli continued to rock them. "But I hope to be as blessed as Levi and one day find a second to love."

Absorbing the fact that Eli was unmarried made her feel a little better about finding him so attractive. Annoying and attractive.

"Oh. Yes, that would be a blessing." Abby swallowed and nudged the rocker to keep her side of the bench moving.

Turning toward her, Eli said, "I understand that your husband also died."

Looking down in shame that she felt anything for this *Mann,* Abigail thought that Abe deserved better—a loyal wife, anyway. "His name was Abraham. Abe."

Of course, Abe had been with *Gott* for years now. Everyone seemed to think she should move on. Thus, Bishop Bechtel.

Eli Probst nodded. "Abraham is a good, strong name. My wife was Joanna. She was killed when our buggy collided with an *Englischer* car."

There didn't seem much to say to this, so Abby just maintained a respectful silence until it occurred to her to say, "You were also in the accident?"

"No," he shook his head, "Joanna was alone, coming home from seeing her sister."

"I'm so sorry."

"*Denki*. It has been years now and," Eli paused before saying ruefully, "I must admit that I sometimes wonder if I actually remember her face. She was a very loving woman, though. That's what I remember."

"I hope to be remembered that way," Abby said. "I think that's more important than remembering how our features are arranged. *Gott* sees the heart. How we behave is most important."

"That's kind of you to say." Eli smiled at her. "How long were you and Abraham married?"

"Five years." She hoped her response didn't sound terse. "You?"

"Three, about."

"Do you have *Kinder*?" Abby supposed she should have asked this before, but he'd never mentioned having children.

"No. None." Eli turned to look at her in the dim light. "You and Abe?"

"No." She tried not to sound as bleak as she felt about this.

He just nodded. "I didn't think I'd seen any little *Kinder* here. Have you lived with your parents since your husband died?"

She nodded. "*Yah*. You?"

"I still have the *Haus* where Joanna and I lived, but when I travel so much, home can be hard to identify. When no one is in it, the place doesn't matter."

Finding herself nodding to this, Abby stared ahead at the sheet of rain.

"Most marry again after they lose a mate," Eli commented. "My *Daed's* been after me about this after Joanna's accident, but

I'm busy with the drilling...and I haven't found another that I want to marry."

It was surprisingly easy to sit here talking to him in the shadows. Abby tried not to be so aware of their shoulders brushing against each other.

He turned toward her again. "The *Menner* around here must be after you."

Abby said nothing about the men in the area knowing she was barren. "I, also, haven't found another I want to marry."

"And your bishop hasn't tried to persuade you?"

Laughing a little, Abby said, "You might not have noticed this, but I can be stubborn."

Eli nodded, smiling again. "I have noticed."

Several days later, Naomi scuffed her way along the lane, some yards ahead of her sisters, Abigail and Faith. The two had lagged behind to look in the culvert at a flower that Faith couldn't identify.

As was common in this area of Ohio, the pastures on either side of the lane were planted with different crops. To her right was a field with tall stalks of sweet corn, tassels waving in the breeze. As she could see a work buggy ahead, Naomi figured it had to belong to someone in the *Gmay*.

"*Hallo*, Neighbor!" Zach Cassel called, grinning as he emerged from one of the rows of corn.

His broad hat tipped back on his head, his blond hair could be seen, plastered to his forehead in the July warmth.

Zach was always grinning. In that way, he reminded her of Eli, the *Mann* drilling their water well.

"*Hallo*," Naomi responded. "I didn't know your *Daed* owned this field."

"*Yah*. He bought it last year."

"The corn looks healthy," Naomi observed, her farmer's daughter background showing.

"It is." Zach looked to where Abigail and Faith lagged behind her. "Are you three out for a walk?"

Nodding at the basket she carried on one arm, Naomi said, "*Neh. Mamm* and *Grossmammi* ask us to pick up some things at Offenthaler's store."

He grinned again. "It's so hot. We should go swimming again at the pond."

Making a face at him, she said, "That was years ago, Zach, when we were *youngies*. We're both grown now."

"We are," he agreed, "but we don't always have to act like it."

By this time, Faith and Abby came along the lane.

"What are you two squabbling about now?" Abigail asked, having come up at the end of Zach's response

"He's just being silly," Naomi said with a dismissive wave of her hand.

"You used to not mind that," Zach observed.

"Back when we were *youngies* and being serious wasn't important."

"*Gott* never said we have to be serious all the time." Zach lifted his eyebrows as if daring her to refute this.

"Come on, Naomi. The two of you used to be such good friends and now all you can do is argue. Come, we need to get these things home to *Mamm*." Abigail took her sister's arm.

What Abby said about them was true, Naomi reflected as her sister marched her down the road. She'd liked being Zach's good friend, but everything was different now. Every interaction pretty much ended in a disagreement.

It was sad, really.

Friday morning, Eli crouched on the ground next to the Zook's old well by their barn, using a pail of water to again wash the mud off the drill stem. As he often did while working, he'd taken off his hat and jacket. This was a rolled-up shirt sleeves kind of job.

About that time, Abby came round the barn from the coop, where he'd heard chickens clucking and crowing earlier. She carried a basket of eggs in her hand. She looked very pretty in her pale blue dress, a shade lighter than her blue eyes, and her white *Kapp*. Just a few tendrils of fair hair had escaped around her face.

Eli recognized that he couldn't have described his own sisters as well, but his reaction to Abby Zook wasn't that of a brother.

She stopped in her tracks when she saw him. "Eli!"

This reaction brought a smile to his face and he said, "*Yah*. I am here."

He readily admitted to himself that his feelings toward Abby Zook were warmer than toward any other *Maedel*. Not since his marriage several years ago, had he felt anything for any other girl. Eli knew that Abby would point out that she had passed the girlish age, but she didn't seem to him like a *Frau* or a spinster to him.

Looking around the shaded area behind the barn, Abby said, "You're here without your helpers?"

"As you see," Eli replied. "They're around by the new well site in the yard behind the *Haus*."

"I'm well aware of the location of the new well," she remarked in a dry voice, walking closer to where he worked. "What are you doing?"

"Washing the drill head clean," he told her. "Here. Would you hold the pipe stem, so it won't move as I work here on the drill head?"

Abby looked over the pipe lying on the grass. "I suppose."

She put down her basket of eggs beside the barn and walked over to help him.

"*Denki*," Eli said. "Hold that end while I clean the drill part and stay there as I work up to clean this part of the pipe."

"Okay." She bent and picked up the end of the pipe section, her blue skirts billowing around her on the green grass.

Eli lifted the drill head over the bucket and scooped water from it to rinse off the mud.

Overhead, a light wind soughed through sycamore and elm tree branches. The silence between them grew thick as Eli moved toward her, washing the pipe that got rammed through the mud in drilling.

"Here," he said in a husky voice. "Move this way and hold off the ground the pipe that I've already cleaned. I'll shift behind to clean that end."

"Alright." Keeping her hands on the pipe, she shifted down toward the now-clean drill head.

Was her voice also husky? Did she feel the tension coursing through the air between them?

Taking the bucket of water, Eli went to the end of the half-clean pipe and started rinsing the mud from the end. As he did so, he cast surreptitious glances at the beautiful blonde woman.

He knew that outside appearance didn't truly matter. *Gott* saw the heart and they were to consider actions more than looks. It was hard to ignore Abby's outward appearance, though.

Each holding their ends, they stood in silence as he worked, moving closer and closer to her end.

An image in Eli's head had him drawn toward her, as if pulled by a rope. He felt that way. Pulled toward her.

"There," he said as he got closer to Abby. "You make sure to keep the drill up. We don't want to have to clean it again. It's heavier than the regular pipe."

"I feel that," she responded, shifting to get a better grip on the drill head.

Finally, he was just feet from where she stood. In his left hand he easily held the now-clean length of pipe off the ground. Working along the pipe, scooping water from the bucket to wash it, Eli finally came to where they stood shoulder to shoulder.

Reaching around Abby, he took hold of the drill head, freezing then. They stood, his arm around her.

To his downfall, she looked up at him then.

Her eyes were so blue and her skin looked so soft. Eli felt himself tilting toward her, falling into those blue eyes until he pressed his mouth on hers.

The pipe fell to the ground, unheeded by either one.

Abby must have been startled because her lips were open and he felt her go completely still. For one fraction of a second, his mouth on hers, she didn't respond.

He needed to stop this, to step way, but he couldn't and, after a moment, Abby started to kiss him back, her mouth moving under his.

At that moment, Eli dropped the pipe he now held and tucked her closer against his chest. It crossed his heated thoughts that, if he could, he'd have stayed like that forever.

CHAPTER FOUR

The next Tuesday, Eli returned to the Binkley *Haus*—where he and his helpers were staying while working in the area—he was surprised to see his *Daed* there, talking to Thomas Binkley.

Eli had been glad to connect that Thomas's wife, Mary, was formerly a Becker and was one of Levi's sisters.

"*Daed*!"

Jobe Probst returned Eli's hug, saying heavily, "It's a nice evening out. Maybe we can talk on the back porch."

Although he was always glad to see his father, the tone in which this was said left Eli with a trickle of dread between his shoulder blades. "Of course, *Daed*."

"Supper will be in about half an hour," Thomas said cheerfully, "don't get so lost in catching up that you miss it. Mary is making brown sugar beef roast!"

"Sounds great," Eli replied, following his father out the back door.

"The drilling is going well?" Jobe asked, seating himself in a rocker on the porch.

"*Yah*. Very good." Eli answered, sitting in the opposite rocker.

"*Gut*," his father said in the same gloomy voice. "Sounds good."

"I'm surprised to see you here so soon after your last visit. Not that I'm not happy to see you. Is everyone at home well?"

"Yes, but I did come to bring some news," the older man said.

"News?" Eli echoed, not worried as his *Daed* had already said the *familye* was well.

"It's joyful news and I know you won't talk of it with pride." Jobe began rummaging in the pouch in which he carried his pipe and pipe tobacco.

"Yes?" Eli waited. This had to be some family news, but he didn't think his father would travel here to tell Eli that one of his sisters was again with child.

"Your *Bruder*, Adam, is to marry this October. Of course, this isn't generally known."

"Of course, not," Eli said, "but this is great news. Not surprising, though. He and Sarah Fox have been going together for several years."

"*Yah*, we all like Sarah," Jobe said, his words not matching his mournful tone, "but it is distressing that your younger brother should marry before you do. You need to marry again."

Eli laughed at this. "*Daed*, four other of my younger *Geschwischder* have married. Since I am nearly the oldest, I always expected that my younger brothers and sisters would marry. No need for me to rush into marriage. Besides, I married."

"*Yah*, and now you have no wife. So sad that the younger of your brothers and sisters marry before you marry again?" his father demanded. "Why should you have expected this? You were widowed and that was sad, but you must marry again!"

Abby Eichelberger's just-kissed image flashed before Eli's mind.

"I will marry again, *Daed*, but I'm still looking for the right woman." Eli rocked back in his chair. "This is no reason for Adam not to marry Sarah."

"No," his father said grimly, "but Adam getting married should be reason to spur you on in your search for the 'right woman'."

"Their moving forward with their lives has nothing to do with my actions," Eli insisted. "Do not trouble yourself, father."

"I'm not troubled and I have turned this over to *Gott*," Jobe assured him in the same grim tone. "But I'm also wondering if I should have given you the company. It seems I may have worked against *Gott's* plan by retiring and giving you a distraction from

31

finding this woman. You know *Gott* has directed us to marry and have *Kinder*."

"You didn't distract me, but you need to let me work this out," Eli assured him. "I'm working on it. I promise."

Having pruned a broken limb off one of their apple trees the next day, Abigail threw these to the side of the garden before she bent to tend to the marigolds along the edge of the kitchen garden. She liked incorporating the flowers, including dill blooms and begonia flowers, as well as squash blossoms in various dishes. The squash blossoms were particularly good in making tea.

Musing that she might experiment with Johnny Jump Up flowers next summer, she didn't at first hear the steps that came up next to the edge of the kitchen garden.

"You have some lovely flowers growing here," Eli commented.

Jumping at the sound of his voice so near, Abigail scolded in a tart voice, "Didn't your *Mamm* ever teach you that it's not nice to sneak up on people?"

"She did," Eli replied with a grin.

Hating that her heart beat faster now, Abigail wondered with frustration why this *Mann* affected her when none of the others around here did. Of course, only a few had shown interest after Abe died. Dinah and Becca might insist that this was because she wasn't approachable, but she knew different.

Would Eli flirt with her this way if he knew that she couldn't have *Kinder*?

"You normally tend the kitchen garden?" Eli leaned against the nearby fence that surrounded the garden.

"Generally, yes. Naomi and Faith often help."

"You have quite a green thumb," he observed.

"*Denki*. We often have enough produce and fruit to sell at our friend's roadside stand."

Abby stood up, turning toward the row of fruit trees behind her. Besides the apple tree, several grew, providing the *familye* with apricots, peaches, cherries and plums.

Very aware that Eli followed her—and that they could be observed from the *Haus* back windows—she asked in a tart voice, "Shouldn't you be digging a well?"

"*Yah*, in a minute," he said, steadying the ladder she'd mounted to reach up to prune some other dead limbs of a cherry tree.

"Hold it steady," she said. "I've almost reached the branch."

"So," Eli said in a warm, teasing voice, "that was some kiss the other day."

Abby stiffened. She didn't know what she'd expected, maybe that he'd be too sensitive to mention that moment. "I don't know what you mean."

"I mean," he said in that same warm voice, "the kiss we shared behind the barn."

"You mean when you kissed me?" she asked, keeping her own voice prim.

"And you kissed me back. *Yah*."

She swiveled around on the ladder. "I did no such thing!"

Eli grinned up at her. "We are talking about the same moment, aren't we?"

Keeping his hand on the ladder, he stuck his head around it to smile up at her. "Are we pretending it never happened?"

Abigail didn't look him in the eye, not answering for a moment. "No Godly woman would kiss a *Mann* she hadn't been courting with."

He smiled again. "Then I guess we're courting."

Now lifting her gaze to his, she said, "I've not agreed to this!"

"Haven't you?"

"*Neh*," she returned, not sounding convinced. "Didn't I hear that your <u>Daed</u> came to see you?"

"*Yah*," Eli admitted. "He came to tell me that my younger brother is to marry this autumn and to push me to marry again."

"That sounds troublesome," she observed. "Perhaps you should think about this more than kissing me!"

"Pass the potatoes," Abigail requested, saying *"Denki,"* when she took the bowl that Naomi handed her. Earlier that Sunday, they'd all been at church. Since the family was eating their meal all together that evening, no one had gone to the Sing.

Even Faith and Naomi were glad to miss this, when Becca and Saul were there. Abby mused to herself that it was endearing to see such a big, taciturn *Mann* as Saul so tender and careful with his expectant wife.

Her heart squeezed a little, seeing the tender moment between Becca and Saul. She and Abe should have brought the first grandchild home to the Zook *Haus*. Them or her *Bruder*, Adam, who didn't seem to be in a hurry to choose a *Frau* from the girls he drove home.

Levi was also there for the meal, smiling at Dinah in such a loving way

His arm around Dinah's shoulder, Levi said in a soft tone, "Your *Daed* introduced me to your well-driller, Eli."

Sitting at the end of the table nearest to her brother-in-law Levi, Abigail was glad the lamp shadows most likely hid the warmth that rushed to her cheeks.

"Oh, yes." Dinah, standing near her soon-to-be husband. "Eli is his name. I was trying to remember it."

"Eli Probst," Abel Zook, the patriarch of the *familye* inserted. "As both *Menner* lost their wives, I thought they should meet."

"Ah." Levi leaned over to kiss Dinah's cheek. "I've been so blessed to have found a new heart."

While her besotted sister responded to this, Abby took a bite of the newly-picked green beans on her plate.

"Abby!" Dinah exclaimed when she finished canoodling with her new husband. "This Eli seems like a good prospect for you!"

Swallowing, Abigail said in as level a tone as she could manage, "A good prospect for what?"

"Don't be silly," Dinah scolded. "As a husband, of course!"

"Why didn't I think of that?" Naomi exclaimed. "Of course, and as you've both lost mates, he can understand your situation."

"I don't think that's a reason to marry a *Mann*," Abigail said. "Sadly, there are others who fit that category."

"That is true," Dinah agreed in a contemplative voice, "Like Bishop Bechtel."

"I think Eli Probst is a better option than the bishop, though," Naomi commented.

"Why?" Dinah asked.

"You will let me know when you two settle on someone," Abigail said.

Dinah dimpled. "*Yah.* Just let us decide."

"May I point out that neither *Mann* has shown interest," Abigail pointed out.

"Well, the bishop has, but I think he's particularly in need of a *Frau*, with all those *Kinder*."

"I think he'd be interested in Abby, even if he didn't have children to look after," Dinah staunchly defended her elder sister.

"Possibly," Naomi conceded, "but I'd think that is a factor for him."

"Eli is better looking—not that this is the biggest issue, but still," Dinah said with a smile.

"He is attractive," Naomi conceded. "I like his smile, too."

With the memory of Eli's "interest" in the forefront of her mind, Abby said, "It doesn't matter because I'm not looking."

If she were, however, she wouldn't dismiss the warmth of his kiss, Abby reflected.

Eli walked around the corner of the Zook *Haus* several days later, headed for the water well location in the backyard.

He stopped in his tracks, seeing Abby coming toward him from the back of the *Haus*. Eli had thought about her and her soft mouth every day since their kiss.

She looked beautiful, her white *Kapp* pinned close to her head, the shadow of the *Haus* blocking the sun's direct rays.

"*Goedenmorgen*, Eli Probst," Abby greeted him, just as if he hadn't held her in his arms not long ago. I noticed that your helpers are in the mess back there. Are you going there to work?"

"*Yah.*"

They were close now, their steps having brought them only several feet apart, face to face.

"*Hallo*, Abby Eichelberger. I've thought of you many times since our last meeting."

Abby looked up at him, her blue eyes considering him. "You shouldn't put any importance on that kiss, you know."

"I shouldn't?"

"No." She came closer. "No."

Eli shook his head. "I really enjoyed kissing you and I'm not kissing anyone else."

From only a foot apart now, she gave him an irritated look. "Well, you probably should because I've never said I wanted to court with you. You are not a reliable *Mann*, from what I see. How many *Maedels* have you kissed in your traveling around?"

"Not many and none in quite some time. Maybe before Joanna. And you haven't said you want to court with me." he responded in a mournful voice that didn't match the smile he sent her.

Abigail didn't believe that he'd made up to no other women since before his wife. He was too playful and teasing! Too flirty!

"You don't speak the truth," she said. "*Gott* has directed us to be truthful, but I think you lie! Look at you. Your helpers go home to their wives and families, but not you. In your traveling around, there are undoubtedly women who flirt back, but not me."

"*Neh*," he said, laughter trembling in his voice, "but you kissed me back."

"Arghhhh!"

Reaching out with both hands, she grabbed him by his shirt and shook him. "You make me so mad! Look, that kiss didn't mean anything. Just like this one means nothing."

With that she reached up and pressed her mouth against his.

Startled for a second, Eli then wrapped his arms around her and drew Abby tight against his chest, tilting into the glory of her body against his, her mouth soft and warm.

When she pulled back a few minutes later, she said in an unsteady voice, "See? It means nothing."

Despite being a friendly guy, he felt no urge to smile at that moment.

His heart beating strong in his chest, Eli took a breath before replying, "*Yah*, nothing. Can we do it again?"

Abby looked around, snapping, "Of course not. I just meant to show you how meaningless this is and don't you go telling anyone about it either. I don't want anyone knowing that I let an unreliable, useless *Mann* kiss me!"

"I have no need to tell anybody about this and I'll just be glad if there's a chance that you'll kiss me again," Eli said.

He wasn't sure what there was about this woman, but Abby made his head swim and he wanted to see where this went.

"Don't count on it," she said in a haughty tone. "You kissed me with no courtship, at all. What kind of *Mann* does that?"

"A brave one," he shot back with a smile. "Would you court with me, if I asked?"

"No. *Neh*, not with a *Mann* who travels around, doesn't ever go home to his *familye* and flirts like you."

Eli just looked at her. She said this, but her kisses said something very different.

He sent up a prayer of thanks that the Zook *familye* had needed a new well.

"I do not believe our meeting was an accident, *Maedel*," he said, not able to keep the husky note out of his voice.

Abby smirked at him. "Just drill the well, Eli Probst. Just drill the well."

CHAPTER FIVE

The next morning, after refilling the oil lamp that hung from the living room ceiling, Abigail came off the step stool, carefully placing the can of oil she'd used on the towel that protected the table there.

She didn't know why she'd kissed Eli the day before. Having relived the moment several times—including the feel of his broad shoulders under the palms of her hands and the warmth of his mouth on hers—she still couldn't figure it out. She also didn't know why she so definitely didn't want others to know.

Everything about him from his smile to his teasing remarks to his kisses with her—a woman he barely knew—indicated that he wasn't to be trusted.

Not that anyone knew she'd kissed him. For some reason, their interaction felt private. She shouldn't have kissed him and certainly shouldn't kiss him again...even though she was very tempted to do this.

Others just couldn't know.

Eli seemed completely interested in kissing her. Just her fortune that he was such a *Mann*. Other *Menner* had shown interest at times, but she'd had no interest in being kissed by them. Her first marriage hadn't been all about making a practical choice. She'd loved Abe. Very much. Loved him still, even though he was gone. Loved kissing him, although he was nothing like Eli.

Why she now felt this marriage thing must be settled like a business contract, she had no idea. She just knew she couldn't stay here, living with her *familye* and hiding out from the world. Bishop

Bechtel did not inspire her to kiss him. Far from it, but he was probably the best husband choice.

A firm knock on the front door just then made her jump. She wiped her hands clean of lamp oil to go over and open it.

There—as if she'd invoked him—was Eli in the flesh. Her heart beat faster as she involuntarily noted that he was all muscled flesh and a bigger amount of it than most.

The tall, blond giant in the doorway said, "Come look at the repairs we made to the back yard. Tell me if we've gotten it right."

"Oh!" Abby blinked, "You're finished drilling the well?"

"Not totally. We've gotten down to the water and we're now building the windmill to draw this up."

"Oh," she said again.

"We still have to fill in the mud pits, but I've laid down some sod over several spots. It's not finished, but come have a look." Eli offered his open hand as if she needed to be pulled toward the open doorway....

Abby let him tow her out the door, down the porch steps and around the corner of the *Haus*.

"I am fully capable of following you," she commented, looking pointedly at her hand, held clasped in his.

Eli laughed before saying, "I guess I like having a reason to hold your hand."

His words warmed her, but she knew she couldn't rely on them. Flirty *Mann*.

By this time, they'd arrived at the back of the Haus. Eli's workers were moving around what looked like a pile of metal at the back of the yard. Closer to where Abby and Eli stood was the new well—and the mud pits he'd spoken about. In front of them, several yards of trampled, muddy grass extended to the back of the *Haus*.

It was at this that Eli waved his hand in a grand gesture. "Behold, the grass is—"

"Still trampled and muddy," she observed.

"Yes, but see the new clean grass?" He beamed at her.

Looking at the several patches of grass—cleaner than the rest—that he'd gestured at, Abby nodded. "Yes, that part does look better than it did."

"See? We are putting it back to rights."

"Don't get ahead of yourself," she said dryly, "Most of it still needs work."

"Yes, Ma'am," he said, looking anything, but abashed. "Shall I come get you when we're ready?"

Three hours later, Abby answered a knock at the back door to find Eli standing on the porch. As usual, he was in shirt sleeves. His blond hair clung damply to the side of his face in a couple of spots and he grinned at her. Also, as usual.

"Ready! He announced. "We got the mud pits filled in. Come tell me how to finish setting the yard to rights."

He said it, Abby observed, as if he were taking her for a drive. As if they were going on an outing.

She wished she didn't feel the same. It was foolish and wrong. Eli had never said anything about wanting to court. Not really, even when she'd brought it up, but still, she followed him onto the porch with a lighter, hopeful feeling in her chest.

If only he was a different type of *Mann*.

An hour later, Eli and Abby sat alone in the improved backyard, his workers having gone to get supplies for the windmill that lie partially built at the back of the yard.

While the grass was still trampled and muddy in spots and the drill pipe jutted from the earth back near the barn, he thought the yard looked okay.

They sat in wooden chairs that sat in the shelter of several tall shrubs—the burgeoning kitchen garden in front of them and the Zook *Haus* to their right. Silence rested comfortably between them as a breeze drifted past.

"Tell me about your husband," Eli said abruptly.

Abby turned to look at him. "Abe?"

"*Yah.*" He'd wondered what kind of *Mann* had won this confident, possessed woman.

"I guess I don't talk about him much."

"Not that I've heard.

She was quiet for a moment before saying finally, "Abe was a good *Mann.* Solid and reliable. Kind."

"What drew you to him?" Eli found himself asking.

Across the yard, rows of plants jutted from the brown soil. He could identify radishes, spinach, green onions and—maybe carrots. The light wind brushed against the leafy vegetable rows.

"I don't know, exactly." Her words were surprisingly honest.

He hadn't actually expected her to answer, expecting a rebuke for his prying.

"We grew up together—the same grade in school, the same *gmay.*"

Maintaining a respectful quiet, Eli waited for her to go on.

Abby reached down from the low chair, tugging at a blade of grass.

"I guess I liked that he listened—like you're doing now—and that he sometimes said funny, endearing things. He never seemed to have a harsh word for anyone." She stopped, making a self-deprecating face. "I'm not like that. Sometimes, I have to work at being forbearing. Abe was that way naturally."

"You must miss him."

The bushes behind them threw shade that reached beyond their feet, moving some in the breeze.

"I do. Even though he's been gone years, I think of him often."

Their conversation felt so easy, Eli was emboldened to ask, "How did he die, if you don't mind talking about it?"

Abby drew in a long breath and let it out. "I don't mind. Others have stopped asking a while ago. He died in a single buggy accident. Those who saw the scene think he must have been driving the buggy too fast when he took a curve. That doesn't sound like Abe, but he was coming home at the end of the day."

Eli registered her calm, low voice and ventured, "You must have envisioned that moment over and over. Like you were in the buggy with him."

"I have." Abby looked down. "I have, but it has been some time, and I must move on."

He looked over at her.

She smiled at the garden.

"The *Menner* around here will probably be very happy to help you with this. I must admit, I'm surprised you've not been snapped up already."

She laughed, the sound dry and brief. "My sisters say that I'm off-putting and that the *Menner* are afraid to approach me."

Turning in his seat, Eli looked at her, demanding, "Surely, not all your sisters say that!"

"*Neh*, but the more direct ones do."

He really had nothing to say to this, as disagreeing with her sisters wasn't a good idea. Eli could see it, though. Abby could be challenging. He liked challenging, though. She seemed worth the effort.

Abby looked off at the rolling fields beyond the kitchen garden. "I need to move forward, though."

"What exactly does that mean?" Eli looked at her unreadable profile, the smooth curve of her mouth and the cheeks with a faint bloom.

"I need to marry again." She glanced down at the grass in front of them. "It is my duty. *Gott* wants us all to raise families."

He couldn't help but be warmed by her saying she wanted to marry again. He knew Joanna would have wanted him to find another loving wife and Eli thought that maybe he might have found the woman for him, but Abby didn't look all that happy when she talked of her duty.

"You don't look happy about this," he pointed out in a tentative voice.

"It's not a matter whether I'm happy or not. I must marry and move forward." She looked over at him. "Do you know Bishop Bechtel?"

Eli thought for a moment. "I believe I have met him. He usually speaks on Sundays. An older *Mann*."

"*Yah*, that's him." Abby drew another deep breath. "His *Frau* died last year and he was left to raise five *Kinder* alone."

"Wow. That would be a lot for a *Maedel* to take on," Eli commented.

"*Yah*. I suppose. A younger woman might seem daunted."

"Not you, though?"

Abby gave a smile that was both sad and determined. "I'm a widow, Eli, not a teenager."

"You aren't that old," Eli scoffed.

"Old enough to consider this."

He frowned. "The bishop has asked you to marry him?"

"Not yet, but he's conveyed that, if I would look favorably on the match, he would ask me." Abby stared ahead.

Eli wondered if the bishop had ever caught her in his arms and kissed her sweet lips. He doubted it. Actually, if he was thinking of the same *Mann*, Eli doubted that this bishop had any passion inside him. Of course, that could be his jealousy rearing its head.

He made himself say, "It's not good to make such a decision in haste."

"*Neh*," Abby agreed calmly. "That's what I think."

"I'm so glad you agreed to drive out with me again," Moses Bechtel said as they trotted along a country lane several days later. "Only last week, my eldest son—Peter—asked if I'd seen you recently. I mean other than at our meetings."

"How is Peter?" Abigaill asked with composure.

"Oh, he's fine," the bishop responded, clucking at his buggy horse. "Only a little irritated that he has to help his sisters with the house chores. Because they're still young and we have no woman in the house."

Abigail noted his heavy hint and merely nodded. "Good. I'm glad he's well."

"Is everyone well at your home? Your *Mamm* and sisters looked very well."

"*Yah*," she said, wondering if every conversation with the bishop would be this dull. Then, she reminded herself again that Moses Bechtel was a good *Mann*, dealing with a difficult life situation.

"It is a fine day, is it not?" He beamed a smile at her.

"Yes, indeed it is. Very fine." Abigail reminded herself that, if she did marry the bishop, there would be the *gmay* to talk about, not to mention matters of home and children.

"Very fine and not too warm for late June," Moses Bechtel pronounced.

The memory flashed through Abigail's mind of having been caught in Eli's arms and kissed till her brain was mush. If she married the bishop, would she still be visited by these thoughts?

The next week's late June sun shone brightly overhead, casting dappled shadows on the slow river from the birch trees that hung over the bank. Naomi sat on the riverbank, a fishing line dangling into the blue-green water from her pole.

Wading in the sluggish river some yards away, Zach said, "I bet I catch a fish before you."

Naomi scoffed. "You don't even have a pole."

"I don't need a fishing pole. All I need are my hands," he bragged.

"This I have to see," Naomi scoffed. "Why are you even here? I came to fish in peace."

"You don't own the river," he said, up to his thighs in the water now. "Just watch this."

"Watch what?" she asked pointedly, registering that her youthful neighbor had grown up a lot in the last few years. He must have worked a lot in the fields with his *Bruders* and *Daed* as those thighs now looked quite muscled, as did his arms. Still, this was her childhood's friend, Zach.

"It looks like you're just standing there," she commented.

"That may be what it looks like," Zach said, bent now with his arms deep in the water. He was very still.

"I can't see much to watch," Naomi commented.

All of a sudden, with a great splashing, he brought his hands up—with no fish in them.

"I can see that's a great way to catch a fish," she commented.

"It swam away fast, at the last."

"Okay. Could you move down the river some? You're scaring away the fish here."

He glowered at her, stalking several feet away in the river. Without a word, Zach slid his hands again into the slow-moving river.

"Maybe that one fish told all the others," Naomi taunted softly after a few minutes.

"No need to waste a perfectly fine worm," Zach responded.

Feeling a tug on her line, Naomi yanked the line in and lowered a wiggling fish into her basket. She said nothing to Zach, knowing he was very aware of her fishing success. Still, he hovered, arms plunged in the river water.

How long they both held their positions, she couldn't say, but she had time to pull in another fish before he suddenly moved like a flash, throwing a fish out of the river, onto the water's edge next to her.

"There!" Zach yelled, splashing toward her while the startled fish flopped around.

Almost as startled as the fish, Naomi could only stare.

"Get it!" he hollered. "Don't let it flop back into the water!"

A half-hour later, the two lie on the grassy riverbank, staring up at the leafy tree branches that hung over the dark green water.

Zach chuckled as he said, "You were so surprised. The look on your face!"

"I'm sure it was no more startled than your face. Admit it, you never thought you'd get a fish like that," she responded, lazily gazing at the one spot of blue sky that could be seen beyond the tree branches spreading overhead.

"I never have caught one that way before, but I've seen it done."

"And how many times have you tried and failed to catch a fish that way before?" she snorted.

Turning her head to see his response, Naomi noted that he shrugged.

"Lots," he chuckled before turning on his side to face her. With several glistening drops of river water in his shock of sandy hair and his smiling, open face, Zach looked not unlike the boy with whom she'd grown up.

Except for his muscled arms—shirt sleeves now rolled up— and broad shoulders. Honestly, Naomi thought to herself, did Zach always look this good?

He turned back to lie next to her. "What's with Abigail and the *Mann* drilling your new water well?"

"What do you mean?" she asked, although she'd also noticed something vibrating in the air between the two.

Propping himself up on one elbow, Zach said, "Don't tell me you haven't noticed. Abigail hasn't given the time of day to any *Mann* since Abe died. She likes this *Mann*. What's his name? Eli?"

"*Yah*. Eli Probst."

"So, what's up with them?"

"I couldn't say," Naomi admitted. "Abigail doesn't tell me her inner thoughts."

"Or what she thinks of this Eli?" Zach concluded from where he lie beside her.

"Neh. I have no idea, except that she…likes him. I think."

At the next church meeting, Abigail looked at the solid *Mann* preaching, knowing he was a good option to help her move on. *Frau* Bechtel. She'd gotten used to being Frau Eichelberger when she'd married Abe. It was the way that a woman took her husband's name. Abigail knew that.

The sermon rolled over her and she heard one word in ten, so lost in her thoughts. She knew she had to marry again. She needed to move forward and no *Mann* had roused in her the feelings she'd had for Abe.

Well, no one but this Eli Probst and she had no idea what that was about. Maybe she felt this way toward him—an even stronger attraction than with Abe—because she had been in this limbo so long.

Eli seemed very interested in kissing her, but he'd never said anything about courting—not really--or marriage and he had no children. How could she carry her infertility into his life?

Bishop Bechtel's five children sat to the side of the crowded room. She knew what marrying him meant.

Her gaze returned to the solid *Mann* at the front. *Yah*, she knew.

There were other *Menner* she supposed. Both Thaddeus Groff and Joseph Kauffman were looking for new wives, as they were recent widowers. Both had big families. Joseph was older—maybe a year or two older than Bishop Bechtel—but still worth considering.

Unfortunately, she didn't want to kiss them, either.

CHAPTER SIX

On the following Monday, Eli held one side of the windmill upright, saying over his shoulder, "*Yah, Daed*. Everything is going well here and I've arranged to dig two other wells while I'm in the area. Several others, as well, are thinking about having wells drilled, so I may be here awhile."

"I'm glad you're getting more work, *der Suh*, but your *Mamm* misses seeing you at home," Jobe Probst said heavily. "You know your *Bruder* is marrying this fall. We'd hate you to miss that Sunday."

The early July sun shone strong overhead and Eli had the random thought that he was glad they had more daylight with which to work.

"Of course, I won't miss that." He braced his foot against the windmill side to keep it from moving as his helper bolted the piece to the next side.

"You know," his father said in a severe voice, "you need to attend to your other concerns. You need to find a wife to whom you will want to come home."

"*Yah. Yah*," Eli said, an image of coming home to Abby playing out in his head. He could kiss her openly, then. He didn't think coming right out and telling her that he wanted to court was the best option, but he was still thinking about it.

How to convince her that he was serious? She'd told him over and over that she didn't believe she was the only *Maedel* he'd kissed and that she didn't think he was reliable.

Pulling a chair forward next to him, Jobe sank into this and Eli was reminded that his father wasn't a young *Mann*.

48

"We have several *Maedels* visiting our *Gmay*. Any of them would make you a good wife," Jobe pronounced.

"Probably not," Eli said with a grin. "I seem to be picky."

Maybe he'd been waiting for Abby. It felt like that.

"You had no problem marrying Joanna," his father commented.

"No, I didn't," agreed Eli, "but my next wife hasn't presented herself yet."

He wasn't sure he said the truth, but he certainly wasn't ready to tell his father about Abby. He had to find a way to get her to think of him as a possible husband.

"No doubt your *Bruder* will want you to be one of his *Newehockers*."

"*Daed*," Eli said, over his shoulder as he turned to face the windmill they were building, "I am only one of Adam's *Bruders*. He's more likely to ask Peter—since they are so close in age—or Matthew, who is the eldest."

"We just don't know. You need to be there, anyway."

With a sudden thought, Eli slewed around to say in an uneasy voice, "Daed, you've not got some girl at home that you want me to court with?"

"Nonsense," his father said, his word completely unbelievable.

Turning back to the windmill, Eli said, "Good. I will pick my own wife, thank you."

"Just see that you do this without wasting more time. You deserve a family of your own," Jobe Probst said.

After finishing holding the sections of the windmill tower, Eli escorted his dad back to the elder *Mann's* buggy and sent him off home. Jobe wasn't so old that he couldn't drive, but Eli didn't want him driving home in the dark.

On his way to the drilling site, he found himself praying, "*Please Gott. Help me know how best to move forward with Abby because I know I want to move forward, but I'm not sure how to do this.*"

Why couldn't this be as simple as it had been with Joanna? Of course, Abby was more complex and seemed stuck in her place. He needed *Gott's* help.

The following morning, Abigail walked toward the river on the way to see Becca. Although she'd wished to have a child with Abe, she had no envy or resentment that her sister was having an experience denied to Abigail. She loved Becca and she was happy for Saul.

Overhead the sky was blue and the breeze blew gently, rippling the treetops and stirring the grass that covered the sunny spots. Near the edge of the river, pickerelweed and duck potato grew and, here and there, blue flag iris sprang up blue blossoms. It was very peaceful with the sound of the river rippling over rocks on the shallow side.

She let her thoughts wander and found herself dwelling on the breadth of Eli's shoulders and the thrill she felt when they kissed. It wasn't good, she knew, but she couldn't deny it. Instead of letting herself dally with a *Mann* who traveled around drilling wells, and who'd be moving on soon, she should encourage Bishop Bechtel. She should move on with her life.

She knew that. Her actions with Eli didn't fit with what she knew was best for her. She didn't for a minute believe that he'd not kissed other girls since his wife passed and he'd probably not even gone home to his Joanna when she was alive.

How could a woman be a *Frau* with peace of mind when her husband stayed away for weeks at a time.

Turning along the edge of the river where it curved, she brushed past a low-hanging oak sapling and then stopped short.

There in front of her, as if her thoughts had brought him to life, was Eli sitting leaning against the trunk of a birch that grew by the river's edge, a fishing line dangling in the water. The tree shaded that side of the river.

Abigail knew she should move forward—or turn aside to go to Becca's another way—when Eli spied her hovering there. He sat up.

"*Hallo*, Abby. You look fetching this morning."

Forcing herself to act as natural as she should—and certainly never felt when she saw Eli—she took several steps forward down a natural decline along the river.

"Eli." Abigail said, pleased that her voice sounded level and natural when her heart was beating at the mere sight of him.

"*Yah*. It is I."

"What are you doing?" She made herself continue to walk toward him.

"Fishing?" Eli said, nodding toward the pole in his hands. "What are you doing?"

His question seemed as reasonable as was hers, she told herself, cringing inside that she asked such a silly thing.

"Going to see my sister, Becca," she answered after a moment.

She came closer, her footsteps muffled on the grass. She peered over into a deep pool at the river edge. "Any luck?"

"*Neh*. Not yet, but I haven't been here that long."

"My *Geschwischder* fish, but I've never learned." Abby paused, making her smile at him as natural as she could. "I don't know why. Always busy with some task or another, I guess."

"Never?" He asked, "Naomi told me about this spot. Surely, your brothers and sisters would have been glad to have you fish with them."

She shrugged. "Probably. I just never have. It doesn't look hard."

"No," he chuckled. "How do you feel about touching worms and slippery fish?"

"I can't say I've had any experience with worms," Abby admitted., "but you have to touch slippery fish to cook them and I've certainly done that."

Several seconds of silence pass before he offered, "If you're not in a hurry to get to Becca's, you could fish right now."

"With you?" She stared at him, a little startled at the invitation.

He pulled his baited line from the water. "Certainly. See? Already have a worm on my hook."

She stood only a few feet from him, at this point, but Eli didn't wait for an answer, reaching out to take her by the arm and turn her once again toward the river.

"Okay." She knew she should march on to see her sister, but she didn't resist him. What was this power the *Mann* had over her? This was ridiculous.

With his cane fishing pole in one hand, he positioned himself behind her. "Here. Put your one hand on the pole like this. And your other hand here—you want a good grip as the fish will tug on the line when it bites."

Abby swallowed, looking at his strong, brown hands covering hers.

Gott, please help me.

"Are you sure you don't want to catch the first fish?" Abby looked up at him over her shoulder.

"*Neh*. I've caught plenty of fish. You try." He stood there behind her, functionally holding her in his arms as they stood next to the river.

She drew in the clean, masculine scent of him, her hands clenching the pole he'd thrust into them. She should be thinking about the unsuspecting fish in the river, but she could only think that she wanted him to reach over, cup her jaw and turn her for his kiss.

It was stupid, really. What future was there here?

"As I have said," Levi volunteered at the Zook Haus the next Sunday. "Dinah has been a blessing to me. Even when she annoys me, she helps me. My shop is better, my life is better. I never thought I'd be so happy after Anna and the baby died."

Eli and he stood outside on the porch before a *familye* dinner the next Sunday at noon.

"I understand that." Eli pondered for a moment. "My *Daed* has been pressuring me to marry again, but I never found a woman I could imagine that with."

"Before," Levi said in a sly tone. "You forget, I've seen you with Abigail."

Eli grinned. "She is a spunky woman. Tell me about your life with Dinah. I don't think you've told me anything, other than her being a blessing."

Nodding, Levi acknowledged, "She is that, but we didn't start off so well. My sister, who had worked with me in my shop, was moving away with her new husband. She asked Dinah to work for me."

Hitching himself onto the porch rail, Eli prompted him, "And that wasn't a good start. You have a kick scooter shop, right?"

"*Yah*." Levi sat across from Eli, in a wooden chair against the wall of the Haus. "We mainly sell and repair kick scooters, and few smaller toys. *Neh*, not a good start because Dinah really didn't want to work for me. She thought I was cold and unfriendly when I returned to town after my first *Frau* died. And I'd stupidly said something mean about Abigail—within her sister's hearing. It really upset Abby."

"What did you say?" Eli found himself bristling in Abby's defense.

Levi shook his head. "I made a remark to some other *Menner* about Abigail's husband having died without a child. It was stupid, as I said. I lost my own *Boppli* when my first wife died. I was wrong to have said anything and I apologized to Abigail."

He grimaced. "She feels bad that she and Abe never had *Kinder*. It's a sore subject and I blundered into that. Dinah understandably held it against me."

"You did have a rough start," Eli remarked. "I can see why you apologized, no matter how you felt about Dinah."

"*Yah*, but that all changed eventually," Levi said, flushing a little. "She's made a tremendous improvement in the shop and...she's helped me be see that I need to act more friendly. It was awkward, at first. She's just been...wonderful."

Eli's new friend then grimaced. "Of course, she still makes me crazy sometimes, but we work things out."

Laughing, Eli nodded. "*Yah*, the ones we love do sometimes make us nuts."

Abby was certainly making him crazy, he admitted to himself. He just had to find a way to help her see that 'moving on' didn't have to mean entering into a loveless contract.

Then, it struck him. Maybe that's what he needed to do—offer her a contract that just seemed loveless. Until it wasn't.

Abigail stepped into the Zook's backyard the next afternoon, a basket full of wet laundry to hang on the clothesline beside the new well, her midsection fluttering. This was silly!

That morning, she'd seen Eli and his workers through the kitchen window, working on constructing something at the top of the windmill tower. She knew he was here.

The laundry had to be put on the line, no matter whether the *Mann* was there or not. It wasn't like she was seeking him out, but she admitted to herself that the likelihood of seeing Eli brightened the afternoon.

Bishop Bechtel and two of his sons were to come by later and she should be glad of this. It just made her clench her jaw with determination. Here was her best choice to move on, yet she hadn't given him a clear message. Abigail didn't know why she'd not done this yet.

There—by the base of the windmill tower—Eli stood. His two helpers were no where in sight.

Abigail took measured steps toward the clothesline, her basket of wet sheets held tight against her hip. She had never felt this mix of nerves and excitement, not even when she was to marry Abe.

"Abby!" Eli called out, striding toward her. "I hoped I'd see you today."

"*Guten Tag*," she responded, aware that her lips curved into a smile.

"Good day to you, too," he said, his own smile broadening.

She set down the basket, standing next to the clothesline. "I came out to hang the sheets. Even though, it's afternoon, they should dry well in this July sunshine."

"*Yah*," he said, bending with her to lift a wet sheet out. "Shall I help? These have to be awkward to hang."

"I'm sure you have other work," she said demurely.

"Not really. Thomas and James are still finishing their lunch at the table on the other side of the barn. I already ate mine. Let me help." Eli flopped a damp sheet over one of the lines that stretched out from pole to pole to allow clothes to dry in the sun.

"I've done this by myself many times," she pointed out, even though she was glad he'd come over.

"I can imagine you have," Eli agreed, "but I'm here, doing nothing. I helped my *Mamm* and sisters do this many times."

"You weren't out working in the fields?"

"Not always," he responded cheerfully, tossing a length of wet sheet over the clothesline. "There were always chores to be done around the house and we *Kinder* did them, as well."

"Here," Abigail said, reaching over to hand him several clothes pins. "Sisters usually do things like hang clothes on the line."

"There are six boys and two girls in our *familye*," Eli said. "We did what needed to be done."

"Good for your *Eldre*," Abigail told him. "Boy *Kinder* can do house chores, too."

By this time, the one clothesline was full of wet sheets, blowing against them when the breeze rose, the sheets filtering the sun. She reached into the basket for the next length of sheet, absently glad to find it wasn't dripping wet.

"Abby," Eli said, shaking out the sheet she handed him. "Has the Bishop asked you to court with him?"

She threw another sheet over the second clothesline before answering, even anchoring it with several pins before saying, "*Neh*."

"But you think he will, when you give him the go-ahead?"

The two of them stood between the clotheslines--as they went down the line, him tossing the wet sheets across the second line and her, pinning these in place.

"Probably. I think so. The only other widows in this town are much older." Abigail stepped past him to shove the last pin over the sheet on the line. The basket at their feet was now empty.

By this time, they'd worked their way to the end of the clotheslines and damp sheets hung on either side of them, blocking she and Eli into a private world.

"Abby?" he growled her name in a low voice.

She looked up at him and he took hold of her pale blue skirt to pull her closer.

Abigail saw the dark emotion in his eyes and let him fold her to his broad chest, raising her face for his kiss. His strong arms around her, Eli smelled of the fresh outdoors and tasted like nothing she could describe.

Sinking into their kiss, her arms linking around his waist. No one could see them, the lines of wet sheets blocking them in and she let herself fall into the heat and sweet hunger in his mouth.

When Eli lifted from her, a few minutes later, his breath coming ragged, he said, "I need to ask you a favor, beautiful Abby."

"You do?" She felt as off balance as he sounded.

"I do," Eli assured her. He swallowed before saying with a tumble of words, "I need you to pretend to marry me. Hold on. Hear me out."

As he'd pressed a long, brown finger against her lips, she paused, confused and still recovering from their kiss.

"You're not in a hurry to court with the bishop and my *Daed* is pressuring me to pick another wife. Let's both take some time to enjoy more kisses like that one. Let's pretend—for a while—that we've been courting and will marry."

"I shouldn't." The words tumbled out of her without thought. She knew what she should do. She should marry a serious *Mann* and get on with her life.

Eli pulled her close. "I'm not saying you won't—if you haven't decided to marry elsewhere—eventually marry a serious *Mann*."

Trying to clear the fog his closeness brought, Abigail hesitated a moment. She so much like kissing him. Eli made her laugh and made her want to be silly—like hiding between the clotheslines to kiss in secret.

"How would this help either one of us?" She couldn't believe she was even considering such a thing, but she was.

"Do you remember that I've told you my *Daed* visited here?"

"*Yah*."

"And that he keeps nagging at me to get married again?" Eli asked, raising his brows.

"Of course, I remember."

"Well, marriage to Joanna was good, but I've not met a *Maedel* that I want to marry now. I don't want to be pushed into marrying until I do. Then, it won't be a matter of 'pushing' me."

Abigail frowned at him. "Didn't your wife die some time ago?"

He nodded. "She did. Four years ago."

"And, in all that time, you've not found another girl you want to marry? Are you still pining for her?"

"*Neh*." Eli bent to gather the basket under his arm, saying ruefully, "As a matter of fact, I'm not sure I still remember her face. I do remember feeling loved, though. I want that again."

Abigail shook her head. "And how would pretending to get married help?"

"It would get my *Daed* off my back," Eli said over his shoulder as they walked toward the end of the clothesline. He paused, giving her a roguish smile. "And, if you'd pretend to plan to marry me, we could kiss anytime."

Just the thought stopped Abby in her tracks.

To kiss him whenever she wanted. Not worried about being seen doing it.

He leaned back, the two of them still sequestered between the drying sheets that hung from the clotheslines. "I know you want to move on and that it seems this Bishop Bechtel is your best option, but why not take a time—a short time—just to do what you like doing? You seem to like kissing me. You keep doing it. Just give yourself a time to do what you like."

Struck by his words and still transfixed by the idea of kissing Eli freely, Abigail stopped before leaving the shelter of the sheets on the clothesline.

"After we end it, you can go back to doing what you think best," he said in a low, seductive voice. "Why not do me a favor and do this for yourself?"

CHAPTER SEVEN

"Abigail." Naomi said that evening. "Abigail!"

Abigail looked up from the pot on the stove that she'd been absently stirring. "Oh! Yes."

"Whatever caused you to drift off like that?" her sister said, reaching over with oven mitts on to scoot her aside so she could open the oven door.

"Nothing," Abby said, moving out of Naomi's way. "Nothing!"

"Her sister opened the oven and a wave of heat filled the kitchen, already warm from the July evening. "*Mamm* just put the green beans and potatoes on the table and *Daed* and Judah are washing their hands. Are the beets done?"

"*Yah*," Abby hurried to assure her sister. "The sauce has thickened fine."

Naomi straightened, balancing the pan that held the roast chickens for their supper. "Faith is out, getting water from the old well. Being so low, getting water from it takes time. The newer, closer one can't be finished too soon."

Abby felt her cheeks flush a little, telling herself that the heat from the oven was the cause, not her sister's mention of the new well, which brought Eli to mind. As if she hadn't been thinking of him and his proposition all afternoon.

She knew that "moving on" didn't involve delaying, which is what she'd be doing if she agreed to his suggestion that they pretend to marry. No, he hadn't actually put it that way, but that was the long-and-short of it.

In an instant, the sensation of being locked in his arms and kissed to distraction hit her like a gust of summer wind. She felt everything all over again, the heat of him pressed against her. The scent of him surrounding her and the feel of his mouth on hers, even as the damp sheets had blown against them.

Gott help her, she'd kissed him back as fervently. Maybe, a little voice whispered in her head, maybe his suggestion made some sense. She'd been here, drying on the vine so long now that Abe was dead and gone. Maybe she deserved some joy. She deserved to be held tight and kissed thoroughly by a *Mann* who'd be gone by the end of the summer.

Bishop Bechtel and his five *Kinner* would still be here in September. She could court with him, even agree to marry him in the fall, after the harvest.

Maybe she should just do something for her? Marriages weren't announced much ahead of the ceremony. There was no need for the Bishop—or anyone—to know that she'd engaged in this pretense with Eli. His *familye*, since that was the point for him, and hers would probably have to know, but no one else. And when Eli ended the deception, no one the wiser, she could marry the Bishop and help him raise his five orphaned children.

As for her *familye*, Abby knew they'd just be glad that she was considering marriage again.

Not since her years with Abe had she felt the thrill of being kissed that way…well, never really. Not even with Abe. Abby told herself she felt that giddiness with Eli because it had been so long.

She'd gone so long since becoming a widow—years. Before now, she'd never even felt a flicker for a *Mann* and, if she was honest with herself, she felt no flicker with Moses Bechtel. He was a good *Mann*, though. She had to give him that.

Dear Gott, she closed her eyes to pray—the kitchen and its inmates behind her. *Please help me to know if this is best. Please help me hear your voice and honor your wishes.*

Other than the reality that she'd be participating in Eli's deception, she wasn't lying herself. If she agreed to his plan, who would be hurt?

"Looks good," Eli pronounced the next day, stepping back from the windmill tower that stood over the new well. He shielded his eyes to look up at the circle of blades spinning at the top of the windmill tower. "I think it's all working right."

"Are we done here, then?" Thomas asked, wiping a sleeve across what little forehead wasn't covered by his hat.

"*Yah*, I think so," responded Eli.

"I'll load the rest of our equipment onto the work wagon," James, his other helper said.

"Do that," Eli responded, "and tidy up the yard as best as you can. We don't want to leave it in a mess."

He felt heavy at finishing here at the Zooks' Haus. Eli had made his proposition to Abby yesterday and she hadn't responded, as they'd been interrupted by her sister.

Truthfully, he didn't think much of his chances. *Yah*, Abby responded to his kisses with enthusiasm, but he knew by now that she was a woman who held herself to a high standard. If she thought she should "move on" and that the bishop was her best option, she'd do it.

He didn't fully know why, but it had been clear all along that she didn't consider Eli an option. Abby had said that he wasn't reliable, whatever that meant. Having reflected on this a lot, he could only surmise that he didn't seem as serious as Moses Bechtel.

Abby didn't love the *Mann*, but she clearly didn't think she could trust herself to Eli. If she'd accepted his plea of needing a "pretend" marriage, he'd have had time to convince her otherwise.

Picking up a rope he started to coil around his arm, Eli spotted Abby coming out the back kitchen door. As she descended the steps from the porch, he became aware that his heartrate picked up, racing in his chest.

She was so beautiful, the sun glinting on her blonde hair where it peeked from her white *Kapp*. He knew from her few statements about her marriage that she'd loved her first husband and he hated that she'd suffered that loss, but determination settled in Eli that, no matter what, he had to convince her to take him as her second husband.

His *Mamm* and *Daed* would come to love Abby, even if she was a little standoffish with them right away.

As she crossed the yard toward him, Eli dropped the coil of rope from his arm and, glancing back to see where Thomas and James worked, he stepped forward to meet her. No matter what she had to say, she deserved the intimacy of them speaking out of others' hearing.

"Eli," Abby greeted him as she got near.

"How are you this morning, Abby?" He asked in what he recognized was a caressing tone.

"I am fine." She looked back at his workers. "Can we speak...alone?"

She could have told him right there, Eli knew, his heartbeat speeding up to a gallop, if she wanted to refuse his request outright. "Absolutely. Let's step around the corner of the *Haus*."

"Fine."

"*Frau* Eichelberger wants to see if we've left a mess in the side yard," he yelled back to Thomas and James.

Seeing Thomas nod in a disinterested way, Eli cupped Abby's elbow in the palm of his hand.

Without saying a word, Abby let him lead her around the corner of the Haus where no one could see them. Without waiting for any comment from her, Eli crushed her to his chest, maneuvering Abby to where her back was pressed to the house and he kissed her, pouring into their embrace all his longing. This might be their last kiss, he told himself. She could become *Frau* Bechtel this autumn and he'd never be able to see Abby again.

He couldn't stand the thought. Eli had to take this one last moment, just in case.

"My goodness," she said when he finally lifted from their kiss.

Both their breathing came ragged and he hovered only an inch above her beautiful mouth, considering kissing Abby again.

This might be his last moment. Their last kiss.

"What was that all about?" she managed.

Not able to form words that would describe the chaos in his chest, Eli just lowered his mouth to her instead, reveling in her leaning up on tiptoe to meet him. Together they clung, kissing, tongues mating until she rocked back, sagging against the *Haus*.

"I only came to tell you," she managed after a few minutes to catch her breath, "that I will help you."

"What?" Eli heard her words, but couldn't register—wouldn't let himself believe—what they meant.

"I will help you," Abby repeated, her beautiful face lifted to his. "Your situation with your *Daed*?"

You will?" He bracketed his hands on her shoulders, his voice exultant.

"*Yah*," she confirmed. "This is only for the summer and you will be leaving here to drill elsewhere when you finish with Grace and Rufus' well."

"I have one other here," Eli confessed, almost afraid that she'd agreed to be courting with him the weeks more that this would take.

"Alright. One more."

He crushed her against his chest again and then bent to give her a hard, swift kiss. "*Denki. Denki.*"

"You're welcome," she said.

"Can my—can my *Eldre* and my one youngest brother come to supper at your *Haus* this Saturday?" Eli rushed to say. "They're coming to see me at the end of this week and—and I'd like to introduce you as my bride."

She hesitated for a moment. "I suppose so. I can tell my *familye* about us this evening at supper. They might be surprised, but not so much as they knew I was determined to marry again. I'll tell them then that your *familye* is coming to supper."

"*Yah*, I think the sooner we do this the better," Eli told her, not able to believe his good fortune. She hadn't agreed to marry him for real. Yet. That was ahead of him, but he felt so joyful that Abby hadn't gone out of his life.

Not yet, anyway.

"So glad to meet you!" Jobe Probst said a week later as he spread a cloth napkin on his lap at the Zook table.

"I'm glad to meet you, as well," Abby said, feeling a little self-conscious.

Along the big table, *Frau* Probst sat next to her *Mamm*, chatting about recipes. Two of Eli's *Geschwischder* sat with Naomi, Noah, Faith and Ezra closer to the foot of the table.

The scene felt strange to Abby, but not as uncomfortable as it should have been, she suspected.

"I should have known Eli had his eye on a girl here," Jobe confided, leaning forward to speak in her ear. "He was always evasive about it, even when I came to tell him of his brother's marriage."

Abby didn't know what to say, and sat, feeling a stupid blush redden her cheeks.

Eli sat to her other side, but she didn't think that he couldn't hear what his *Daed* said, there was such a hubbub of chatter in the room. He must have had some intuition, though, because he reached over just then—beneath the table—to cover her hand in her lap with his.

Turning her hand in his, she clasped it and felt strangely comforted. When she agreed to this subterfuge, she hadn't fully thought out what all it would mean. Thinking back, when she and Abe had told their parents that they'd agreed to wed, the families had met to eat together. Not having met Eli's *Eldre* before as they lived in another county, she just hadn't thought about this.

Sitting up a little straighter, it occurred to her then that her sisters would expect to help her make a wedding dress. This lying was insane! She'd never not told the full truth to her *Gershwischder* and her *Eldre*!

Taking advantage of Jobe Probst talking to her *Daed*, who sat at his other side, Abby leaned over to hiss to Eli, "This is out of hand!"

"*Neh*, we're all right, *Liebling*," Eli murmured, squeezing her hand.

Startled at his use of the affectionate term, Abby decided to ignore it, hissing, "We're lying! To our loved ones!"

All because she liked kissing Eli, a little voice reminded her.

"*Shhh*," he hushed her. "We're committing no sin. They are all happy and—when this is all over—no one will care."

Falling silent, her hand now lax in his, she reminded herself that she'd always planned to marry Moses Bechtel in the coming fall when Eli would have moved on. Because marriages weren't talked about beyond immediate *familye*, no one would know that their union had even been discussed.

Certainly not Moses Bechtel.

She didn't want to hurt anyone.

"I must get inside!" Abby said, pulling out of Eli's arms the next Sunday. They'd snuck into a corner next to the Bachman *Haus* chimney to melt into one another's arms. "The service will start soon and we'll be missed."

Eli watched her go, his arms feeling empty already. In the week since she'd agreed to a "pretend" engagement, he'd come to wonder how he was going to get her to agree to really marry him.

How did he get Abby to see that he was a reliable *Mann*?

"I'll go first," she told in in a low voice. "You come into the *Haus* in a few minutes. The preachers will start speaking in a few minutes."

"Fine, *Leibling*," he said, thinking a tender word now and then might start her thinking of him as a long-term option.

"Stop calling me that," she admonished in a scolding voice. "Particularly where you might be heard."

"If anyone saw the two of us speaking in a secluded spot like this, I don't think they'd need to overhear me calling you sweetheart," Eli teased, holding on to her hand to the last minute as she started toward to front of the *Haus*.

Abby flashed him a chiding look before disappearing from his sight.

Dear Gott, he prayed, stepping back to lean against the Bachman *Haus,* "*Help me know what to do. I love Abby so much. I want her as my Frau, my reason to go home between jobs. You see the future as I can't. You know best, always. Help me convince Abby to marry me.*"

CHAPTER EIGHT

"Your *Bruder*, Peter, finishes up at the Neff farm soon. I thought he might come work with you afterwards." Jobe Probst announced while sitting on the front porch swing of the Binkley *Haus* that evening,

"That's a good idea," Eli responded. "It will be good to work with Peter."

"Well, son," Jobe said after a moment, "I think your Abby will be a very good wife for you."

Leaning against the porch rail not far from his *Daed*, Eli smiled. "You do?"

"I do. I like her very much."

Eli's *Mamm*, Rachel was in the kitchen with Mary Binkley, and his two *Bruders*, Adam and Peter, had gone to the Sing at the Bachman *Haus* that evening.

The two men—father and son—were alone on the porch.

"I'm glad of that, *Daed*. I'm glad you like her," Eli told him. He'd been trying so long to earn his father's approval—now that the business had been passed on to him—but he found that he no longer cared about that. "I'd marry Abby regardless, but I am glad you like her."

"I thought there was a reason you were staying her so long," Jobe said in a sly voice, not even blinking at Eli's declaration.

Eli looked down. He was more sure of his desire to marry Abby than of anything in his world. This pretend thing might keep her from marrying another *Mann* right now, but he was more convinced as he sat here on the porch rail that he had to make a push.

At least, he thought this was the right thing.

Please, Gott, he prayed, *help me convince Abby that I am the right Mann to marry. That I love her and I will be the best husband for her.*

"*Yah*," his *Daed* said in a satisfied voice, "both your *Mamm* and I like her and think she's the best *Maedel* you could have found. She has a nice *familye,* too."

"I think so," Eli confirmed.

Maybe, this was *Gott's* answer.

The next Friday, Abby sat with her *Mamm* and *Grossmammi* Ruth next to the campfire while Naomi and Faith rummaged through the food stuffs they'd brought as they prepared to make a stew.

Overhead, the breeze fluttered the leaves on the beech and maple trees, moving the branches when a current of air came through.

"I'm surprised you could tear yourself away from Eli so soon to go camping," her *Grossmammi* commented with a sly smile.

"Not at all," Abby said. It wasn't necessary to have a campfire in late July, but the crackling blaze made such a lovely sight. "Getting outside to enjoy these woods is always nice."

"Besides," Faith put in from over by the camping table, "Eli is coming to visit Abby here."

"*Ahhh,*" *Grossmammi* said with a laugh.

"Stop teasing Abby," *Mamm* said when their chuckles subsided. "We're all glad she found the right *Mann* to marry."

As the others fell into chattering about various things, Abby was silent, struggling with guilt over this pretense. Faith was right. Eli had told her—having learned that she was going camping in these woods with her *familye*—that he also was camping there with friends.

She should have known that Eli had made friends with whom he could camp. With the side of her mouth quirking, Abby noted to herself that he was a very friendly guy, after all.

"Do you think that you and Eli will marry this fall?" Naomi settled into a camp chair near hers.

Abby stared into the fire. What had she been thinking? To lie this way to all her *familye*! Just for a *Mann*.

Who kissed like sin. She should have known to avoid this—sinning with him.

"I suppose so," she answered her sister.

"I bet Eli will find wells to drill in this area," Faith said, teasing as she poked at the campfire with a stick.

"His *familye* live in Hocking County," Abby said, not fully answering the question. Because theirs wasn't a true engagement, she supposed neither had thought it necessary to specify this.

"I suppose it doesn't matter where you live as Eli travels all over, digging wells," Faith said, flopping onto a rock that faced the campfire. "What do you suppose Noah, Ezra and *Daed* will bring home for supper?"

That was another reason not to actually marry him, Abby thought, attending to her sister's earlier remark. Eli was rarely home.

Naomi, who'd gone back to look through the food crates they'd brought, now responded to Faith, "They went fishing, I think."

Just then, Eli erupted from the undergrowth near a beech tree. "*Hallo*, Zook *familye*!"

Despite herself, Abby felt her cheeks grow warm.

"See," Faith murmured to her, "I said he'd come."

"Where did you spring from?" *Grossmammi* Ruth asked. "We didn't see anyone else here when we drove into the campgrounds."

Stopping beside the old woman to drop a kiss on her withered cheek, Eli said cheerfully. "I'm here with the *Hausers*. We just drove in a half hour ago."

"I didn't know you knew them," Naomi commented, having pulled from the food crates the food stuffs they'd need to fry whatever fish her *Daed* and their *Bruders* brought back.

"Oh, yes," Eli responded, "we met at the services."

It was completely natural, Abby knew, that Eli made friends so naturally. Did he find girls to kiss wherever he went? She was reserved and his outgoing outlook seemed foreign to her.

"We're so glad to see you," her *Mamm* said, rising to give him a hug.

While they talked, Abby tried to quiet her guilt. Her *familye* all liked Eli so much that they would all be very disappointed when the arrangement came to an end. To say nothing of their distress when she married Moses Bechtel, instead.

"Come for a walk with me."

Eli broke into her thoughts with his warm invitation.

Her quick glance around at the others encircling the campfire found that they were all smiling and nodding.

"Okay," she said, rising from her seat.

Naomi grinned. "Supper won't be ready for some time. You are, of course, invited, Eli."

As Abby walked away with him—his hand holding hers—she asked, "Won't the *Hausers* wonder where you are?"

"*Neh,*" Eli assured her. "I told them that I was going over to visit friends."

"At least, we don't have to tell them of our broken engagement."

"We wouldn't, anyway," he reminded her. "This kind of news is never shared until right before a couple marries."

"Of course."

"Come," he said, drawing her into a dense clump of maple, oak and rlm trees.

Abby let herself be pulled into the thicket of trees.

"Finally," he said, "I haven't kissed you for days."

With these words, Eli settled her against a broad Oak tree trunk and bent to kiss her senseless.

Letting herself fall into the heat, Abby yielded to his temptation. Knowing that they couldn't be seen, she looped her arms around his neck and kissed him back with matching urgency.

This pretense might trouble her in ways, but she was in. She might as well revel in the benefits.

He was warm and the clean smell of him drifted up from his broad chest. His tongue tangled in hers and Abby knew then that this was something she'd never before experienced. She'd been kissed, but never with such ardor, such total enveloping passion.

When they'd both drawn back with ragged breaths, he clutched her to his chest and Abby found herself blurting out, "This must stop!"

"What do you mean?"

She took a deep breath, saying in a hard voice, "Only that we will have to stop this eventually and...doing this now...will only make stopping doing it later hard."

The smile Eli sent her was crooked. "Don't underestimate yourself, Abby. You are a very strong woman. You can stop whatever you think best."

Her pulse still drumming in her veins, she responded, "Not this. I don't think I'm that strong."

"Eli is so attractive," Faith said a week later, smoothing her hand over the blue fabric Abby had reluctantly chosen for her wedding dress.

It would do for her eventual wedding to Moses Bechtel, Abby had thought when her sisters pushed her to make a dress.

"I don't understand," Becca said, rocking slowly in a chair nearby, "why you were so hesitant to have us help with your wedding dress."

"Well, it could have something to do with you being so near your time."

"Don't be silly," her sister replied, smoothing a hand over her very rounded belly. "That has nothing to do with this. The baby isn't due for a month"

Abby threw an amused glance her sister's way. "I actually don't need a dress. I still fit the one we made when I married Abe."

Her comment drew a cacophony of response from her *Schweschders*.

"Of course, you can't wear the same dress!" The youngest of the sisters, Faith, seemed horrified by the thought.

"No! Why, you're starting a new life with Eli," Dinah pointed out, reaching out a hand to nudge Becca back into the rocking chair.

"Your dress for your upcoming wedding to Levi is already finished and hanging on a peg. It's natural that you're excited for your marriage. I've already done this once before," Abby pointed out, wishing the subject would change to anything else.

She didn't want to think about any of this—saying goodbye to Eli…marrying Moses Bechtel. None of it. She almost hated the blue fabric they kneeled over now.

It made no sense as this was a lovely blue, the color of flowers that spread over the fields in spring, and she believed being married to Moses wouldn't be terrible.

"I like that Eli smiles so often," Naomi said, turning her head away from the fabric to look at her sister. "You need someone to make you laugh, Abby."

"She laughs," Dinah reproached their younger sister.

"Don't squabble," Becca said, laughter trembling in her voice as she held her belly.

"You know what I mean," Naomi said. "You've said that Saul settles you down. It's always good to have a mate to balances you."

"I did say that," Becca admitted, "and Saul is much more steady than me."

"But that's not to say that you can't be steady," Dinah insisted. "Just as Abby can laugh."

"Of course, she can," Naomi smoothed the fabric out for cutting. "I never meant that she couldn't. Just that Eli will help her see the humor in life and this is good."

Abby said nothing, wondering if Bishop Bechtel saw any humor in life. She'd never seen it, if he did.

"I never thought I'd like Levi when I started working at the shop," Dinah volunteered out-of-the-blue. "Sometimes love surprises you."

"Not always," Naomi said practically. "Lots of couples we know met in school."

Abby looked at her two sisters with a frown. "Dinah, when did you first know you loved Levi?"

"It was several things," Dinah said, leaning back on her feet from where she'd crouched on the floor in front of the fabric. "He was so different with the *Kinder* that came to the shop. Not cranky or mean, like I'd thought he was. He even let one teach him to play a game--that he already knew, but he wanted the boy to feel good about it."

She smiled at the memory. "Then, he 'helped' me when I needed to talk to someone who was objective about the *Menner* I was considering. He was helpful, but he really wanted me for himself."

"Of course, he did," Becca said with a smile.

"Abby," Faith interjected. "When did you know you wanted to marry Eli?"

"*Yah*, sister," Naomi seconded. "Eli's not the sort of person I'd have thought you'd fall for."

"What does that mean?" Dinah jumped in, ever defensive for her elder sister.

"Hush," Abby put her scissors down and rested her hand on Dinah's arm. "I have been...serious, I guess. Eli's not the most obvious choice."

"So, why did you choose him?" Faith said again.

Feeling her cheeks turning red, Abby searched for a reason she could offer her sisters. She couldn't say that his kisses had swayed her, intoxicated and enraptured her.

"It's obvious why Abby fell for him," Becca scoffed. "He's very nice and he's nice looking."

"That's what I said," Faith confirmed. "And he likes us. He REALLY likes Abby."

"How can you see this?" Abby blurted out the question. "I mean, in what way."

"Well, to start," Naomi offered, starting to cut the fabric, "Eli asked you to marry him."

"There is that," Dinah agreed, "although lots of *Menner* would do that, if she'd ever indicated interest. I can also see it in how Eli is always where you are."

"And he touches you a lot," Becca inserted. "On the shoulder and taking your hand. I've noticed. Saul does the same."

"Of course, he does," Naomi said, "he's naturally more protective now that you're with child."

"He did this before I was with child." Becca rolled her eyes.

"He did," Abby said, speaking up to soothe the disagreement between her sisters.

"Those are only some of the ways Eli shows he likes you," Faith said, bending over to smooth out the length of blue fabric for her sister's shears. Doesn't he show you his feelings when he kisses you?"

"Kisses don't mean a *Mann* wants to marry you," Dinah said in a dry voice. "I know."

"Maybe not," Naomi spoke from her spot on the floor, "but I wouldn't think a *Mann* just wanting kisses would look at a woman the way Eli looks at Abby."

"He looks at me a certain way?" Abby asked. She hadn't thought of this.

"*Yah*. Like he wants to marry you and to whisk you away," Dinah said, from beside Becca's rocker.

Of course, Abby reflected glumly, he could be doing this in front of the families to support their lie.

She hated that thought.

The next morning, Abby left the house early with most of her *familye* slumbering. She knew she shouldn't have left Dinah and the others to fix breakfast, but she needed a walk to clear her head.

Swishing though the long grass in the field closest to the *Haus*, Abby sighed.

Yesterday—making her wedding dress with her sisters—had left her with a turmoil of emotions. For one thing, it felt wrong to even make this dress as it was for a sham wedding that would never take place.

Even though the dress could be used when she married next, she supposed.

For another thing, she found herself continuing to imagine what it would be like to actually marry Eli.

And this would never do. He'd always been a flirty *Mann* who moved from town to town in his work and he'd never tried to hide this. Although he'd had one wife, he'd never taken another, despite all the pressure he got to do so.

He'd never hidden that, either.

The folded blue fabric on the table in her room seemed to mock her after her sisters had left for the night.

She sighed again now, trailing down to sit on a rock near a small, bubbling stream.

To see Eli's laughing face across the breakfast table.... To welcome him home each Saturday evening.... And those kisses.

She acknowledged to herself that she wanted these things. Wanted to be with him, to feel his arms around her always.

Abby wiggled her white *Kapp* to settle an itch on her head.

She couldn't deny it. She'd fallen for those kisses with Eli and foolishly warmed thinking about holding his hand. This was stupid, but she'd played over her sisters' chatter when cutting out the pieces for her wedding dress.

She had to admit to herself that she'd fallen in love with Eli.

Even though, she prided herself on her practicality and she knew the foolishness of falling in love with a flirty *Mann* who traveled around for work, Abby had to admit that she loved him. She loved Eli...and now she had to be stoic when she married another *Mann* after she and Eli "broke up."

She didn't know how she was going to do this.

CHAPTER NINE

"Psst!" Eli whispered several days later.

Abby looked up from the spot where she sat, weeding the plot of garden behind the Zook farmhouse.

"Eli!"

Her surprise was understandable as he hadn't said when he'd be back from his visit home to attend to business.

Now, he stood at the corner of the *Haus*, beckoning her to come to where he stood. He was so happy to see her that his heart thundered in his chest.

She looked beautiful, even in her patched dress, smudged with dirt from the garden, her golden hair tucked up under her white *Kapp* with untidy tendrils escaping.

Looking mystified—and chillier than she had recently, he noticed—Abby stood up, shaking her skirt free of garden dirt.

She crossed the yard, shaking her head as she neared him. "We don't have to sneak around you know. Our pretense covers all this."

As she neared the corner of the *Haus*, he reached out and drew her into the shadow of the structure.

Yielding to a powerful urge, Eli pressed her back against the tall bulk of the *Haus* and bent to kiss Abby thoroughly. To his deep joy, she threw her arms around him and rose up to press her body against his. His eyes closed to focus on the sensations of her—the heated silk of her mouth, the warmth of her body, the curves and valleys--Eli pushed her back more firmly, molding her between the *Haus* and his own tense body.

Their mouths mated and he reveled in the taste of her on his tongue. Oh, Abby.

Moments later, he lifted from her, lifting a hand to frame her face in his grasp. Both breathing heavily, Eli spoke after a moment. "I've missed you."

"You have?"

He could almost see her backing off.

"I have," he affirmed. "And I'm very glad that you missed me, as well."

"What makes you think that I've missed you," Abby responded, a shuttered expression in her eyes.

"Your kiss," Eli responded with a smile. "I can't imagine that you greet all with that passion."

She pushed his hand away from her face and moved several steps away. "It's all well and good for us to act a couple in front of our families, but I don't think we should do so when we're alone. Not anymore."

His gaze resting on her, his heart still pounding, he asked, "Why not?"

Her expression almost stern, Abby looked down. "We never planned this to go on forever. If it is to end, we should start getting used to being no more than acquaintances."

Taking the plunge, Eli blurted out, "What if we don't end this?"

He hadn't planned out what to say or even that he'd propose this morning. That's what this felt like, a proposal.

Abby looked up at him. "I don't know what you mean."

Moving toward her to take her hand in his, he said, "Why don't we marry? Actually."

Not responding immediately to his words, she just stared at him.

"Abby, I actually do want to marry you," he told her. "I'm not pretending. Will you? Marry me?"

Staring at him in shock, she said stupidly, "What?"

In the last few days, Abby had thought many times about marrying Eli for real, reveling in his strong arms about her always, but his offer startled her. Abby had never expected this. Not really. He wanted to actually marry her?

"I want to marry you," he said, as if he'd heard her unspoken question. "To spend my life with you. To come home to you when my work allows. To have *Kinder* with you."

As she stared at him still in speechless shock, her brain not able to form words, Eli declared, "I love you, Abigail Zook Eichelberger, and I want to marry you. I want to kiss you forever."

Trying to assimilate his words, her hand still resting in his, Abby stared at him. The thought of him wanting Kinder with her brought everything to a halt.

When Abe had suggested they marry, it hadn't come as such a surprise. They'd been courting for months and he'd recently joined the church. It had been time for him to marry.

"I think," she said, remembering all the heated kisses she'd shared with Eli before her concern about his flirting nature slammed into her thoughts. "I think you can't be serious."

Abby withdrew her hand from his, propping both fists on her hips.

"I am," Eli assured her sincerely.

"I have seen you with all the other woman here, Eli Probst."

They stood still in the shadow of the *Haus*, the sun overhead, but not yet casting down its noon rays.

"*Yah*? What have you seen?" He seemed puzzled.

"You tease and joke! You laugh and play!" Abby insisted as they stood several feet apart, her stomach now churning.

He shook his head. "I may do all this, but none of it has anything to do with whether I want to marry you."

"You move around for your work, drilling wells all over. You rarely go home to your *familye* and you probably even drill for *Englischers*."

A smile again curled his mouth. "Of course, I drill wells for *Englischers*. They pay good money for the work and, yah, I drill wells all over. This has nothing to do with us. I've rarely gone home because I have no wife and *Kinder*. No *familye* of my own.

That's what I want with you. Give me a reason to go home. Marry me."

All Abby could do was stare at him, turmoil and uncertainty filling her. That, and longing. She so wanted to believe him, to fall into his arms and forget anyone else.

"You are right," Eli replied, reaching out to again snag her hand. "I have traveled all over and met many Maedels. You know my father has remarked on this, but I assure you, my lovely Abby, that never before have I wanted to marry anyone the way I want to marry you."

Feeling herself melt inside at these words, her stomach starting to churn for a very different reason, Abby let him draw her forward.

"Please say yes," Eli murmured. "I want to shout it from the rooftops—although I can't because everyone already thinks we are to marry."

His wry comment drew a chuckle from her and she didn't resist Eli drawing her into his arms.

"Say you'll marry me," he instructed. "Please marry me."

Her head filled with fuzz and unable to believe that she was getting just what she'd longed for, Abby said, "Yes. I'll marry you."

Eli pulled her closer, emitting a triumphant crowing noise.

A hand against his broad chest, even as she registered the heat of him, Abby directed in severe tone, "You must promise to come home every night."

Gathering her close, he promised, "I will. Whenever I'm within a buggy drive distance and when I'm working further away, I'll take days out of drilling, just to come home to you. I can't wait to have you welcome me home."

The next morning, Abby sat behind the counter at Levi's kick scooter shop while Dinah rang up a *Daed* and his son.

When her sister finished, she came over to hoist herself onto the high stool next to Abby. "I'm so glad *Mamm* and *Grossmammi* dropped you off to visit while they went off to shop."

Abby reached out to squeeze Dinah's hand. "It's good to see the two of you working here."

Levi was outside, in front of the store, watching several of his *youngie* customers show him the tricks they'd learned on their scooters.

"I know it means a lot to Levi that you came to visit, he still tells me how bad he feels that he made that unkind comment about Abe. And where you could overhear him!"

"I've told him several times that I forgive him," Abby said in a composed voice.

"I know," Dinah returned, "but he still feels bad about it."

"He's just hoping that you've forgiven him," Abby told her. "Once we are brother and sister, he won't be as worried."

"Maybe not," Dinah agreed, growing pink at the mention of her marriage. "Do you think you and Eli will be married this fall? I can't see why you'd wait."

"I don't know." Abby felt herself flushing at this. She was still getting used to the reality that Eli wanted to marry her for real! It seemed startling that he thought that he loved her.

Her earlier doubts about his flirty and his moving all around to work still sometimes whispered in her head, but she just pushed all that away.

She wasn't prone to emotional decisions and she tried her best to be practical, but all that seemed to have gone out the window as Eli had wormed his way into her heart. When a *Mann* kissed a woman so passionately, it was hard to think at all.

"Oh, look!" her sister exclaimed then, pointing at the shop's front window. "Eli is here now."

Looking up quickly, Abby saw Eli exchange a few words with Levi before he stuck his head in the doorway.

Abby took several deep breaths and tried to calm the sudden thunder in her chest.

"*Hallo*, my beloved and her sister." He waved at them cheerfully.

"*Hallo*," returned Abby, not unhappy with his term of affection, but not used to it, either.

"*Hallo!*" Dinah smiled at him, looking satisfied with his display of affection.

"I've come to pick you up. I met your *Mamm* and *Grossmammi* in town." Eli beamed at them.

Feeling her own cheeks grow warm, Abby managed to say, "Okay."

"I'll be outside here with Levi for a few moments" Eli said, gesturing at the tall Mann surrounded by *youngies*. "We'll leave after that."

Abby swallowed, momentarily overcome with happiness. "Okay."

"He's such a nice *Mann*," Dinah pronounced with approval. "I'm so glad you're marrying a happy, laughing *Mann*. I worried that you'd end up with an older serious type."

Her sister made a face. "That's all we seem to have around here."

Laughing, Abby said, "Now that you're marrying Levi."

"*Yah*," Dinah agreed, chuckling in response. "He was the last of the young, lovely *Menner*. At least, until Eli came here."

Abby idly watched the group out the front window. "I have faith that our brothers and sisters will find partners.

Six or seven young boys formed a group around Eli and Levi, all seeming focused on the boys' kick scooters.

As Dinah chatted away about her upcoming nuptials, Abby noted that one of the *youngies* had talked Eli into letting the boy teach him to ride a scooter. It was difficult to imagine that a *Mann* as fun-loving wouldn't have already learned this somewhat-risky skill, but Eli mounted the boy's scooter, bending to listen to something the boy said.

As she watched, her heart beginning a slower thumping in her chest, Abby felt herself growing steadily more absorbed in watching their interaction. Eli was so open, his face so kind as he listened to his young instructor.

He seemed absorbed and the *Buwe* looked as if he loved it.

Eli Probst was good with children.

Why hadn't she thought of that? Children and Eli. When he'd asked her to actually marry him, she'd only thought of how much she loved being with him. How much she loved him.

Sitting there watching him playing with the *Kinder* around Levi, the blood seemed to leave her body. She felt cold and filled with a profound sadness.

The realization slammed into her--she couldn't marry Eli.

Couldn't deprive him of having children of his own. In all their talk, Abby hadn't ever told him she was barren. She hadn't felt the need. Their wedding was never going to happen, she'd thought. She'd planned to marry Moses Bechtel when their farce was over. A *Mann* who already had *Kinder*.

She saw now that she couldn't marry Eli, no matter how much she loved him. Because she loved him, she couldn't marry him. He'd said that he loved her, too, but would he still if years passed and no children were born to them?

How could he not feel cheated, especially since she knew that she was barren. Abby looked through the kick scooter shop's big front window and acknowledged to herself that marrying Eli would mean cheating him out of the *familye* he wanted. She couldn't take away his hopes and dreams.

How could a person do that to the Mann she loved?

Just as she admitted to herself—Dinah sitting a few steps along the shop counter—that she couldn't marry Eli, Abby realized how difficult it would be for her to tell him. How could she end their plans to marry when she loved him so much? And he'd professed that he loved her.

"I need to leave!" she blurted out. "I have to go."

Dear Lord, she prayed, alone in her room that night, *"Dear Lord, tell me what to do. I love Eli so much, love kissing him, love having him make me laugh. If I do this, if I marry him with him still not knowing that I'm barren, he will come to hate me. He'll never kiss me or try to make me laugh again.*

I will be stealing away all his hope and all that he dreams of. His Daed gave the drilling business to Eli and he'll need a son to pass it along to. I would be so selfish to deprive him.

Help me, Lord. What must I do? I don't want Eli to hate me.

She knelt on the rug beside her bed, glad that her sisters hadn't come into the bedroom yet. Abby could hear them chattering downstairs as they cleaned the kitchen.

All through the evening meal—all through the drive home with Eli—she'd held her tongue, nearly silent and making herself smile at appropriate moments. Eli had questioned her, seeming to know she was troubled and pulled inside herself, but her *familye* had made no comment.

Abby was aware that her *Mamm* and several others in the *familye* had cast concerned looks her way. She could only be relieved that no one had said anything.

She was so troubled in her heart that she couldn't have said a word to comfort them, never mind comforting herself. She didn't think she'd ever feel anything other than grief.

Please help me, God. Comfort my soul. Hold me in your arms and make me okay with living my life without him.

For I know what I should do.

Two days later, Becca pulled a tray of freshly baked cookies The windmill creaked as it spun overhead as Eli and his crew gathered their tools in the Zook backyard, loading these onto their work wagon as they prepared to move to the next job at Grace and Rufus Bassler's *Haus*, only several fields away.

He turned his head toward the backdoor, thinking he'd heard it open. His heart beat faster at the possibility that Abby came out to see him.

Eli loved her so. As they drove home from the kick scooter shop the day before, he'd told her that they'd be in her backyard early, loading their tools onto the work wagon.

He thought he saw her in the dawning morning light, her graceful figure descending the porch.

The morning air was cool, blowing gently as he watched her cross the yard. In the dim light, he could see her moving toward him as he stood by the work wagon next to the new well windmill. The men's voices could be heard along with the spinning windmill and Eli's heart swelled at the site of her.

He smiled at her, stretching out a hand to her.

Abby smiled back and Eli felt his heart contract at the sight. She stopped several feet away and waited where she was while he came forward.

"*Hallo*, my beautiful," Eli said in a low, caressing voice as he came near her.

"Please," Abigail said, putting her hand out to stop him.

"What? Are you not well? You should be in your bed," he scolded. Now that the morning light was coming up, he could see that she did look pale.

"I am not sick." She looked down at the ground between them.

Taking a step closer, he asked, "What is it then?"

Eli moved to gather her into his arms—he knew they didn't have to worry about his workers seeing them, as he had his back to Thomas and James and his bulk would block them from view.

As he moved closer, however, Abby stopped him, her hand flat on his chest.

"I cannot marry you," she rushed to say, her words tumbling out in a scatter. "I am serious and you are not. You aren't reliable and serious. You are flirty and you travel all over, never going home. I see now that I cannot marry you."

Staring at her in the dim light, Eli said in a startled voice, "What?"

"I cannot," she repeated, taking a step back from him, saying in a hard, gasping voice. "I've thought it over and prayed about it. I can see now that we should not marry."

"Are you sure you're alright?" Eli asked again, his words tender. "This is all nonsense."

Abby said, "I'm fine and I'm sure about this."

Eli stepped forward to take her hand. His words were low and teasing. "Sweet, wonderful girl. You cannot mean this. You're worrying and stressed. There is no need. We will do very well together."

"Eli," she said in her most 'Abigail' voice, "I cannot marry you. It would be wrong. Believe me in this."

Staring at her, stunned and distressed as her words sunk in, he could say nothing.

"I will marry Bishop Bechtel!" she announced with a touch of defiance.

Slowly shaking his head, Eli said, "You cannot mean this."

Dread filled him and he tried to convince himself that she didn't mean what she said. Only, he could think of no other reason she might say this.

How could she marry Bishop Moses Bechtel when she loved him?

"I do mean it," she insisted. "I need to move on and the Bishop is a steady reliable *Mann*."

"Which I am not?"

"No," she barked at him. "I am convinced that you're not. Hopefully, Bishop Bechtel and I can be married right after the harvest season. He and his *Kinder* need a woman in the home."

"Abby," he said, angrily, "you love me. How could you marry another?"

He stared at her with a mixture of bafflement and frustration. "You could not kiss me the way you do and not care."

"Of course, I can," she insisted, sounding more and more flustered. "*Menner* do it all the time."

"Well, I don't!" he cried.

"I cannot stand here arguing with you," Abigail cried. "Believe me or not!"

Turning on her heel, she stalked back to the *Haus* and he stood there, looking after her, feeling like he'd been run over by an *Englischer* car.

All Eli could manage to think was thank *Gott*, he didn't live here. His travels took him all over the surrounding counties and, because he loved Abby so, he didn't want the pain of seeing her every few days.

After the Bassler well was finished, Eli would move on. He may have other wells to drill in the general area, but he'd not see her as often and he'd make sure not to go to services here.

The thought of not seeing her both distressed and relieved him.

Eli suddenly craved the comfort of going home.

CHAPTER TEN

"She is the cutest *Boppli* ever," Saul cooed the next day at the newborn in his arms.

"Well, I'm glad she finally made her entrance," Becca said, seated in the nearby rocking chair in the bedroom she shared with her husband.

"We all are," Dinah agreed. "Can I hold our little girl, Saul?"

"Yes, don't hog her," Faith teased.

"The child is his after all," Naomi commented in a dry voice as Saul handed the baby to Dinah.

"Hold her head," he said directed.

"This isn't the first *Boppli* I've held," Dinah returned, speaking low and soft.

Abby commented, "Definitely not the first. She holds all the babies she can."

"I'm glad you two decided to name her after Saul's *Grossmammi*," Mary Zook said, gazing at the baby over Dinah's shoulder.

"The name Ruth just seemed to suit her," Becca observed, readjusting herself in the rocker, "and we loved that we could honor Saul's grandmother. She was so kind to him."

"It is a lovely name," Abby agreed with a smile, determined not to let her own struggle show on her face. She'd cried herself to sleep last night, grieving the loss of Eli and his teasing smiles.

She loved him, that's why she'd done what she knew she had to do.

"Is nursing going okay?" *Grossmammi* asked, as Dinah handed the baby back to Becca.

"So far," Becca assured her.

"She seems to have more than enough." Saul stood next to his *Frau's* chair, looking awkward, but earnest.

Becca and Saul's bedroom was crowded with Zooks, even Abel was there, the patriarch of their *familye*.

Abby looked around the room, sending up a silent prayer of thanks to *Gott*. She had so many blessings. The room was full of them...but she couldn't deny the heaviness of her heart. This *Boppli* was so welcome, so cherished. Little Ruth. Abby ached that she couldn't have *Kinder* of her own, but she could share in caring for her *Geschwischder's* children.

"You look like you could use another pillow," Naomi said, handing Becca one as her sister prepared to nurse the now-fussing *Boppli*.

"Shift the pillow under your arm," *Mamm* directed, bending over her daughter to adjust the pillow.

"I'm so glad you could all come visit," Becca said when her child had latched on. "Even you came, *Daed*! And you're in the middle of harvest time."

Abel scratched his bearded chin, "We just started harvesting. This was worth the time."

Listening to them talk, Abby reminded herself again that she had no room in her life for sorrow. The gap that had been left by her sending Eli on his way would soon be filled...she hoped.

Dear Gott, Abby prayed at church the next Sunday, *please help me. This knot in my chest won't go away. I know that ending things with Eli was for the best—for him—and still I cannot stop crying.*

The Ramseyer *Haus* was hot, even though all the windows were open to let in air. At the end of August, warm weather was to be expected, even as fall ventured forth with cooler evenings and mornings.

Blinking her tears away now, Abby's head bent as Moses Bechtel prayed at the end of his sermon, she surreptitiously whisked away the moisture with her finger.

To her dismay, Eli occupied a seat with a group of *Menner* across the room. How was she to keep her composure when she saw him even here. She'd not thought out that he'd be in the area still, while he drilled a well for Grace and Rufus.

And here he was. If she looked up, she'd meet his gaze.

Keeping her head bent in what she hoped looked like a devoted posture, she prayed over and over for *Gott's* grace.

She was determined, however, that her hesitance with the Bishop had to end. Today, after the service, she would smile at him and encourage him to eat with her *familye*. She needed to move forward and Moses already had *Kinder*. Not having more wouldn't be a great loss for him.

This had to be done. She couldn't continue living with her *Eldre*, drying up like a raisin. At least, she could be of service to the Bishop's children.

If Eli would only go away.

She knew the scent of the Bishop, when he held her close, would be different. She knew the smell of his sweat would not be Eli's scent. This should comfort her. She'd been married before. Abe had his own smell and for weeks after his death, she'd slept with one of his shirts.

That had been a long time ago, however, and by the time Eli had swept her into a hot, earthy kiss, she'd registered only him.

As the Bishop's prayer droned on, Abby could only hope that the memory of Eli's scent would drift away in time.

Walking through the woods two mornings later to Becca's *Haus* to help Naomi and Faith help Becca, Abby came to an abrupt stop as she crested the slope beside Rush Creek.

Eli. In the river pond. Naked to the waist.

Abby stopped, frozen by the unexpected sight of him as he stood at the edge of the pool.

She swallowed hard.

Of course, Abby knew that the creek ran along the bottom of the pasture behind the Bassler *Haus* and she knew, too, that he was drilling a well for Grace and Rufus. She hadn't known, however, that she'd find Eli swimming in the pool that Rush Creek provided before meandering along its path.

Naked to the pants, his shirt discarded on some nearby bushes.

Never had she felt more awkward.

"Abby!" Eli exclaimed.

Her brain seeming at a full stop, she just stared at him.

"What are you doing here?" His question wasn't particularly smart, but he seemed as dumbfounded as was she.

All Abby could do was stare at him, her foolish eyes drinking in his well-defined chest muscles and his tight stomach. She knew she should say something, but she couldn't.

This was surely not the first time she'd seen a man almost naked—her brothers and her husband, of course—but stupidly, this was the first time she'd stared so openly.

"I took a few minutes to cool off after the drilling at Rufus and Grace Bassler's *Haus*," Eli gabbled, running a hand nervously through his wet hair."

Finally finding her voice, Abby managed, "I'm walking this way to Becca's *Haus*. She had her baby."

He'd held her with those muscular arms, her mind registered, and these were the wide shoulders she'd clung to when being kissed breathless.

She felt breathless now.

"I should be walking on. I'm headed to help Becca," Abby repeated, hardly knowing what to say. She should leave, she knew, but here her feet were rooted.

Still standing in the river pond up to his thighs, Eli stared back at her.

She had the mindless urge to wade in and kiss him until the water around them sizzled—but she didn't.

"I should go," Abby said again.

"I wish Becca and the *Boppli* well," Eli managed, his voice sounding hoarse.

"I'll tell them," she said before wheeling around to leave. "I'll tell her."

Eli didn't know why he was torturing himself by staying in the area—going to church where he was assured of seeing her.

Climbing the rising ground above the pool in the river, he wiped his shirt over his wet hair and berated himself foolishly. If Abby wanted to end their engagement, she wasn't likely to change her mind. He should give Rufus and Grace a reference to a man he knew that could drill their well.

There was only heartache here for him, Eli reflected as he stalked over the field that led to the Bassler *Haus*. Staying near her wasn't good for him.

Why did he keep putting himself through this? Seeing her was agony.

CHAPTER ELEVEN

"I made the right choice," Abby told her *Mamm*, trying to settle the uneasiness in her stomach. Her mind kept wandering to that image of Eli's glorious form.

She gulped.

Her *Mamm* and Abby sat in chairs brought out to the backyard, snapping peas for dinner.

"No one has the right to make your decision about a possible mate," her *Mamm* said, shadows cast on her by the tree branches blocking the afternoon sun.

Abby looked at the beloved face, age starting to blur her *Mamm's* features.

"I shall marry an older *Mann*," she insisted doggedly. "A *Mann* like Bishop Bechtel. Someone widowed who already has *Kinder*."

"Of course."

Her mother cast her a searching look that Abby decided not to notice.

"I don't want to marry a flirty *Mann* who travels all over the county and rarely goes home." She bent over the pan in her lap, the snapped green peas blurring a little with moisture she quickly blinked away.

"No?"

The single syllable question brought her head up. Abby gave her *Mamm* a searching glance. "Do you think I'm wrong? I should I marry Eli?"

It was stupid, but she almost wished someone would talk her into marrying him, even though she knew it wasn't best for him.

Her mother released a deep breath. "It just seems that if you were actually interested in marrying Bishop Bechtel—or another older, widowed *Mann*—you would have invited one of them to eat with us. Let him drive you home or out for air, that's all."

"Oh." Abby knew that she should smile more at Moses Bechtel. Start something with him if she was to move in that direction. "I'm just trying to let this thing with Eli settle. You know, if the news of our engagement has spread to others. I think I shouldn't be seen as jumping from *Mann* to *Mann*."

"*Neh*," her Mamm agreed, "only it's unlikely that anyone else—besides *familye*—knows you were planning to marry Eli."

"His *familye* knows," Abby reminded her, feeling a little desperate to justify her delay.

"And they live in another town. They do not have many acquaintances here. Remember that they told us that when they came for supper?"

"*Yah*." Feeling increasingly hollow inside, Abby could only bend her head again over the pot of snap peas.

After a few minutes, she blurted out, "It was not in Eli's best interests to marry me."

Her *Mamm* paused to stare at her, no longer snapping peas. "What do you mean? How can this be the case? He loves you and you love him."

Hearing her *Mamm* say this so simply, Abby couldn't deny the truth of her words.

"Doesn't *Gott* want us to be loved and to marry a partner that will be by your side all your days?" Her *Mamm* asked, bending once again over the bowl of peas she snapped in half.

"*Yah*, He does, but he has also told us to go forth and bear *Kinder*. You know I cannot. I am barren. I cannot deprive Eli of having his own children."

Glancing up to see the look of astonishment on her *Mamm's* face, Abby watched the older woman set her own pot of snapped peas on the grass next to her chair. She reached over to place her hands over Abby's.

"How can you say this? You and Abe were only married a short time."

Abby vented a scoffing laugh. "*Mamm*, some *Fraus* are with child before they've been married six months."

"Some," her mother conceded, "but not all. Don't you remember the story in the Bible of Sarah and Abraham? She never thought she'd have *Kinder*, but *Gott* knew this was best."

"*Mamm*," Abby said in a hard voice, "I cannot rely upon *Gott* to open my womb. He can do this, but this could be the burden that I bear. Perhaps, I am to be the sheltering arms for the Bechtel orphans."

"*Yah*," her Mamm nodded. "That could be, but only if you love Moses Bechtel with all your heart."

Abby said nothing, a lump in her throat precluding this.

"Do you love him? Moses, I mean."

Although Abby kept her head bent over her bowl of snapped beans, she felt her *Mamm's* searching look.

"I don't know Moses well enough to answer that," Abby returned in a hard voice. "He seems like a nice enough *Mann*."

"I think he is," Mary Zook agreed, "but you've not chosen to get to know him...and describing him as a 'nice enough' *Mann* isn't saying much."

"*Mamm*," Abby said, "*Gott* has directed us to be kind—to love—our neighbors. My marrying Eli would not be...kindness."

"I tell you, Zach," Naomi declared in a waspish tone later than day, "that you cannot truly know you want to join the church if you don't take a *rumspringa*."

Forking hay into the feeder for their horses, Zach said over his shoulder, "I already know what I want, Naomi. Why should I go on *rumspringa* to decide?"

"You cannot know," she informed him, "until you see the other world."

"I have seen enough of how *Englischers* live." He bent to snag some hay that floated on the water in the drinking trough. "The tourists that come this way have shown this clearly. I also have *Englisher* farmer neighbors. I don't want that life."

"I don't believe any of us know that world until we live in it," Naomi declared as if cinching an argument.

"And your rumspringa to work at your aunt's bed and breakfast helped you decide whether you want to join the church?"

"*Yah.* It did, and I think you're risking realizing later if you missed something if you don't take time away from this spot."

"You're nuts," he scoffed, hoisting himself onto the fence rail next to where she stood. "I'm perfectly happy here."

"How can the *Maedel* you want to take as wife know that you won't change your mind and abandon the church?"

Shifting on his seat on the fence rail, Zach scoffed, "I think that you, Naomi Zook, just like to boss people around."

"I do not!" she disagreed with heat. "I know of just such a case, although this Mann did take a rumspringa and ended up leaving our life."

"We all know of those cases," Zach said, "that's why *Eldre* recommend their *Kinder* to take rumspringa."

"Well," she pounced, "don't your *Eldre* want you to do that?"

"My *Eldre*," he said in a lofty tone, "trust me to make the best decision for me."

"I don't see how you can do this if you don't have all the information," Naomi said with asperity.

"You just want a break from me while I go away," Zach teased.

"Don't be silly."

Zach said sadly, "You want to be friends with Tim Bomberger. You think I'd just get in the way."

"No, you wouldn't," Naomi refuted in a disgusted voice, "and I think Tim Bomberger is a *Bisskatz*, which you know."

"He will inherit his family farm."

She ticked off on her fingers, "One, that isn't for sure. Two, I really dislike Tim Bomberger, so his having a farm wouldn't matter. Three, you're inheriting your family farm, so I might as well court with you."

Heaving a deep sigh, which Naomi knew was still in jest, Zach said, "I'm glad to know I rank higher than Tim, who you don't like."

"You could at least go to the next county and visit your cousins!" she said, returning to the original topic of their conversation.

"I do visit them sometimes," Zach said calmly, "and this is not for *rumspringa*. How would that be stepping into the other world?"

"You could get a job there!"

"I cannot think why," he said, sending her a puzzled look, "you want to send me away. Are you telling me that you no longer want to be friends?"

"No! It's because I am your friend that I want you to truly know what you're choosing."

"I do know, I assure you," Zach told her. "I want this life. Here. I will join the church and be happy and faithful."

"*Hhmmpf*!" Naomi growled in frustration.

"You are miserable, Abby," Dinah said later that afternoon. The two sat at a round table beside a living room window, stitching on Dinah's wedding dress and the new white muslin *Kapp* she was to wear the day she married.

Not responding to her sister's comment, Abby lifted the *Kapp* in her hand and said, "You will look lovely in this. I think white becomes you."

Laying aside the blue dress, Dinah reached for Abby's hand. "Tell me about your troubles, *Schweschder*. The reason you gave us for not marrying Eli seems thin."

"I don't know what you mean." Abby's hand that held the new *Kapp* sank to her lap. She wasn't used to being questioned in her choices, but she was too unhappy to speak in an outraged tone. Instead, the words came out flat and she heard it herself.

Light streamed through the large window to their right and the cheerful voices of Noah and Ezra could be heard as they exited the kitchen to head back to the north field after their lunch.

"Please," Dinah said, tugging gently on the hand she held. "You said nothing at breakfast or lunch and you haven't talked much for days. You're miserable. Why did you and Eli break it off?"

"There are not to be questions about these things." Abby tried to inject some animation in her denial. At least, she could work at being believable.

"We are sisters," Dinah reminded her unnecessarily. "How could I not notice your unhappiness?"

Lifting her gaze to her sister's, she said nothing, a sudden lump in her throat blocking words.

Abby supposed she should have expected something like this from Dinah. She'd always been closest to her, even though she loved all her *familye*.

She swallowed, knowing that Dinah was likely to say the same thing as *Mamm*.

"I saw Eli playing with the *Kinder* at Levi's shop." She looked down to the *Kapp* in her lap.

"And?"

"And he was so happy, so wonderful with children he'd just met." The words exploded from Abby, "I couldn't do it! I knew I couldn't marry him!"

To her own dismay, she burst into tears.

Shifting seats to be next to her, Dinah hugged her and Abby sank onto her shoulder and wept. Emotion clogged her throat as she thought of never seeing him again, never being swept into his arms. Never kissing him again.

"Sister, sister! Do not cry. It cannot be as bad as you think. Did you and Eli fight?" Scrambling in the pocket of the dress she wore, she dug out a square of white cotton and offered it to her sister.

Wiping ineffectually at her wet cheeks, Abby took the handkerchief that Dinah offered and used it to mop up the dampness that kept falling. Finally, she just pressed the hanky to her eyes. "I love him, Dinah! I love Eli too much to do this to him."

"To do what to him?" Dinah cried. "He clearly loves you, too. How is any of this a problem?"

Taking a deep breath to still her hiccupping sobs, and again pressing the now-damp handkerchief to her eyes, Abby asked tiredly, "Did you not hear what I said?"

"*Yah*, I heard you. I just don't understand."

With a final scrubbing at the tears on her cheeks, Abby said with deliberation. "I was married before, Dinah. For five years. And I have no *Kinder*."

"Oh." Dinah sat back in her chair. "You ended things with Eli because you don't think you'll give him children? That's what you meant about having seen him playing with the *Kinder* at the shop."

"Yes," Abby said in a dull voice. "I love Eli and I cannot allow him to marry my barren self."

Dinah asked gently, "Is this not his choice? If you even are barren."

"What will he say? He is a kind *Mann*. He will marry me, if I accept him, but he will grieve this all of his life."

"You do not know this," Dinah insisted, "just as you do not know that you are barren. Five years is nothing in a life. Maybe you will become with child if you were to marry Eli. It is possible that Abe had a problem or that the two of you together couldn't conceive, but you can with Eli. Either way, you both are miserable without one another. Isn't this something?"

Eli sat on the swing on the Binkley's front porch the next evening, gripping with his right hand one of the chains that held the swing, as he solemnly watched the late August sunset. The heat of the day was waning and the air a little lighter, but he barely noticed. He supposed that autumn would come soon and the leaves on the trees would start showing yellow and orange around the edges.

The others were inside still eating supper, but he needed to be by himself.

Without much interest, he saw that a black buggy turned into the Binkley drive.

Letting his gaze brood on the buggy as it came to a stop on the gravel sweep in front of the *Haus*, Eli was startled when Levi Becker swung down from the vehicle.

"Eli!"

"*Hallo*," Eli returned. "What are you doing here?"

"*Hallo* to you, too," Levi said as he strode up toward the house.

Eli muttered, "I didn't mean it like that."

"Friend," Levi said, mounting the porch steps, "why are you frowning at me?"

Looking out over the front yard, Eli said, "I'm not frowning."

He knew he didn't wear his usual genial expression, but he just didn't feel capable of this. Just as he hadn't been able to leave this area, even if that would be better for him.

"I came to talk with you," Levi said, dropping onto the swing next to Eli and making it sway awkwardly for a moment.

Eli just looked at him as his statement didn't seem to need a response.

"We've been busy at the shop. I only just heard from Dinah that you and Abigail broke up."

Again, Eli could only look at him. He dug wells. He could talk about that, but he didn't think he could talk just now about Abby.

He missed her so. Not going to church services, not running into her in town or at a local pond, didn't help. He still missed her,

"I know these things aren't to be talked about outside of *familye*," Levi commented, "but you know I'm about to become *familye*?"

"*Yah*. Abby told me. I wish you and Dinah well."

"*Denki*. I wish you the same."

"How can you say that?" Eli almost snarled.

Levi put up a hand. "Just listen to what Dinah told me."

"Alright," Eli responded in a calmer tone.

"Abigail told Dinah," Levi said, "and Dinah told me—she said I can tell you as she can't--that Abigail still loves you."

Knowing he still frowned at the *Mann* sitting next to him on the swing, Eli took a breath before saying, "I believe this, but she said she will marry another *Mann* instead."

Hearing this from Dinah via Levi should have made him happy, but nothing changed as Eli saw it.

"Do you know why?" Levi's voice was gentle.

Feeling his shoulders sag as he repeated Abby's words, Eli told him. "She said something about me being flirty and traveling around too much."

Levi waived a dismissive hand. "Abigail didn't give you the real reason."

"What?" Eli growled. "That cannot be. I've never known a more truthful woman in my life. Including my own *Mamm* and sisters."

"You're right, overall," Levi agreed, "but Abigail has a reason why she didn't say the truth."

"Why would she have ended our engagement then?"

"She's in a bad spot. She loves you too much to marry you."

Eli declared, "You make no sense!"

"You know that Abby was married before."

"*Yah*, I do. Of course."

Levi took a deep breath, "To my good friend, Abe. They were married for five years."

"*Yah*?" Eli looked at him blankly.

"And they never had *Kinder*. Abby is convinced this is her fault and that she cannot give you children."

Comprehension dawned. Eli took a deep breath and released it. "*Ahhhh*. I remember you telling me that she was upset when she overheard you having said something about her husband dying with no children."

"*Yah*. She did get upset, because this is a sore subject for her." Levi went on, "She saw you playing with the children at my shop. Remember? We were outside with a bunch of them."

"I do remember." Eli stared in the space in front of the porch swing. In some ways, this information made his situation worse. She loved him…enough to let him go.

And she was convinced that she couldn't have children?

Eli stared in the blank space in front of him.

The question was—did he want to leave Abby to find another woman, somewhere, who could give him *Kinder*?

CHAPTER TWELVE

"Abby! Have you heard?!" Faith gasped several days later, holding her side as she tried to catch her breath.

Abby looked up from the vegetables she was chopping on the kitchen countertop. "Heard what?"

Her younger sister didn't answer immediately, clearly still trying to catch her breath after rushing into the *Haus*.

"Did you get everything from the market?" Abby looked over at her, still chopping the carrots before her.

"*Yah*, everything," Faith assured her. "While I was at Offenthaler's store, I ran into Rachel Bechtel, Bishop Bechtel's eldest daughter."

Flushing at the mention of the Bishop's name, Abby bent over her chopping board, "*Yah*?"

She needed to invite him to lunch. Needed to smile at him more and encourage him to drive her out on buggy drives. If this was to be her future, she needed to stop stalling the inevitable.

Thoughts of Eli needed to be pushed aside. Abby was sure she could do this. She'd grieved Abe in silence, she needed to do this with Eli.

Although he was alive and still working in the area, she had to push aside all thoughts of him.

If she could.

"Rachel and I have become friendly," Faith said, pulling over a kitchen chair and flopping down on it. "You will never guess what she told me!"

"*Neh*, I cannot guess," Abby responded in a matter-of-fact voice.

"You know we are directed not to mention others' business, marriages and the like."

"*Yah*." She looked at her sister with curiosity.

"Well, Rachel was so excited that she had to tell someone! Her father, Bishop Bechtel is to marry a woman—Hannah Brenneman—from Hocking County. You know, the county just south of us?"

Stunned at this news, Abby could only say, "Yes, I know Hocking County is near."

Rather than feeling irked that the *Mann* she'd resigned herself to marry was to take another woman as wife, she was flooded with relief.

"Are you sure?" she turned back to the carrots. "It isn't good to receive gossip about someone else, but if you do, you certainly want to make sure you heard correctly!"

"Oh, yes. I heard correctly." Faith snuck a carrot slice from the chopping board to munch on. "Rachel went on and on."

"Oh, well, good for the Bechtel *Kinder* and for the Bishop, too."

Faith, leaning against the cabinet next to her, frowned. Wasn't he interested in you? Before you agreed to marry Eli?"

"You know that's all off and Bishop Bechtel only spoke to me a few times." She hoped her sister wouldn't notice the rapid reddening of her cheeks at Eli's name.

She had to stop blushing every time he was mentioned!

"*Yah*, I know you aren't planning anymore to marry Eli," Faith said, casting her a curious look, "although I can't see why. He was perfect for you."

"Never mind," she pushed aside her sister's fingers as the girl reached out for another carrot slice. "This is not your business."

Grabbing a piece before retreating from the counter, Faith commented, "No, but it's sad that Rachel is freer with her information—to an acquaintance—than you are."

Two days later, Eli toiled in the Bassler backyard, between his work activities, his thoughts always returning to Abby and what Levi had said.

She still loved him. He didn't know what he should do.

Thomas tossed him the pick that his helper had used to dig the bigger mud pit.

Catching the pick, Eli held it while Thomas positioned himself to straddle the small ditch they'd dug. Reaching out, he signaled for Eli to throw it back to him.

Doing this, Eli stood by, holding the dig pipe with the drill bit attached. When the pits were done, they'd raise the tower in place and start drilling.

Eli knew these steps like the back of his hand. He'd worked with his father, doing all this from a young age. It was like second nature by this time which let his mind wander...to Abby.

His first reaction was joy that she loved him. He missed her so much he ached with it.

Her low laugh. Her silken lips when she quickened to his kiss. He loved the smell of her and sometimes he'd now turn in the midst of his work, sure that she was behind him.

Still, he knew that he had to listen to the concerns that had led her to break it off with him.

Eli did want *Kinder*.

He didn't know how to resolve this. Maybe she was wrong about not being able to bear children—

"Boss!"

Thomas' call broke into his thoughts and Eli pushed them aside to focus on the job at hand.

Later that afternoon, as he climbed into his buggy in the sinking sun, Eli found himself praying. He'd been so distracted and so distressed that he'd forgotten that he was not alone in this. *Gott* was with him.

Setting his buggy horse on the road to the Binkley *Haus*, he fell into prayer. Silently, Eli ignored the ripening field he trotted past and lifted his thoughts to Gott.

Dear Blessed Lord,

Help me. I don't know what to do, Lord. I want to go to Abby and tell her that I love her and beg her to marry me, but is that fair, Lord? I love her and I don't want to come to resent her for us not having children. She told that she planned to marry a Mann who already has Kinder.

Maybe I should let her. She will not be resented, but respected for all that she will give them.

Only I love her, Gott. I have been alone since Joanna died. You were with me as I grieved her loss and I went on with my life. I worked, Lord, and I looked, wherever I went, for a woman who I could love. I tried to carry on, Gott, as you would have us do.

I found no other woman, though. No other Maedel who warmed my heart. I know that you desire us to have a helpmate and to live productive, fruitful, loving lives. I have tried to do this, but I do not know how to leave Abby behind.

Please help me, Gott. Please.

The next day, Abby went with her *familye* to services. She sat next to her *Mamm*, fanning herself in the early September warmth as they sat in seats at the back of the Denlinger *Haus*, she focused her eyes on the Bishop as he spoke.

The room had fallen into respectful silence when he'd stepped up to offer the main sermon.

When she looked at Moses Bechtel, Abby realized she felt no loss. Faith's news, the other day, had come as a surprise, but not a disturbing one. In fact, Abby was glad that Bishop Bechtel's *Kinder* would now have a mother. From the smiles the Bishop exchanged with a woman who sat at the front, Abby could see that he was pleased with his choice.

That this left her with no path to move forward, should have distressed Abby, but it did not. At this moment, she could not imagine being with any *Mann*, but Eli. Her heart was his and if she died without marrying again, she would do this.

She ducked her head then, praying thanks to *Gott* that she had loving *Eldre* who housed her and never pressured her to marry again and leave their home.

Even when a different bishop had come to see her only six months after Abe's death, her parents had stood by her insistence on staying single in her grief. Now that she put her memories of Abe in a quiet corner of her heart, she fallen in love with Eli. His genial smile and his soul-stirring kisses.

Eli, who flirted with other women. Eli, who moved and traveled around for work.

He'd never made her doubt his loyalty or his sincerity. Even when they'd only pretended to be together to keep his *Daed* from harassing him, Abby had known that he'd done that for his father's peace of mind. It had benefited Eli, but Jobe Probst had pushed his son to marry again for Eli's sake. He'd worried for his son and Eli had acted to put his father at ease.

Tangled in her private thoughts, she could only be grateful that Eli hadn't come to the last worship service.

The image of him from when she'd stumbled on him, rising from the pool in the woods, a sudden, unexpected, heart-stopping sight, rose up in her memory and Abby pressed her eyes tight to keep from leaking a tear.

She was doing this for Eli. It was because she loved him and knew that he would be a loving, wonderful *Daed*, it was because of this that she'd decided not to marry him.

Later, as she helped serve the meal following their meeting, she carried an empty breadbasket back to the kitchen, when Levi Becker appeared at her elbow.

"Abby!" he said in an excited voice, "I have something to show you. Come this way."

Although Levi had made a hurtful comment in her hearing—prompting Dinah to be angry with him—Abby had long ago accepted his heartfelt apology. He was to marry Dinah in only a month. Abby was glad for him and Dinah.

"Can it wait, Levi? I have this basket to take back to the kitchen."

"No," he insisted, clasping her elbow to urge her to the side of the Denlinger *Haus*, "bring the basket and come this way. It can't wait."

Urged forward and confused, Abby could only suppose that Levi had some surprise for Dinah that he wanted her sister to approve.

Rounding the corner of the house onto a grassy patch that was hidden from view of the front and back yards, she saw a lone *Mann* standing there.

Eli.

Looking behind her, she saw that Levi had disappeared and before she knew it, Eli had stepped forward.

Thrown off balance by this unexpected development, Abby could only utter, "What are you doing here?"

She hadn't seen him at the service, which made his sudden appearance more startling. Not that she'd admit to having searched the Delinger living room for him.

"I came to see you."

Eli stood in front of her, beautiful to her eyes and she could only drink in the sight of him. She should turn and go back to the others. She shouldn't be here with him.

Abby knew she was weak.

"Don't be mad at Levi for bringing you here," he begged, "I asked for his help."

"I can't think why." Although she'd seen him at meetings—and in that one memorable moment at the river pool—they hadn't talked. He hadn't tried to engage her attention.

"Don't be mad at Dinah, either," Eli directed. "It's only natural for a *Maedel* to talk with the *Mann* she plans to marry."

"Dinah?" Abby echoed blankly, her mind racing to consider what her sister may have said.

"*Yah*." Eli stood before her, holding her hand in his. "I told Levi how upset I have been to have lost you."

This startled her further. "You did?"

"I did and he told me that you told Dinah that you still love me."

She felt the heat run to her cheeks. "Levi had no right to discuss this with you!"

Eli took and released a deep breath. "Possibly, but he saw that I was suffering."

Standing there in the shadow of the Denlinger *Haus*, she could only echo, "Suffering?"

"*Yah.*" He took another breath. "Levi also told me why you ended our engagement."

She swallowed, turning to leave, emotion clogging her throat. "I cannot talk with you about this."

"Please stay," Eli said. "Please don't disappear into the *Haus* and sneak away."

Abby snapped. "That you think I would do that should tell you something."

"It does. It tells me that you love me and think that us marrying would make me unhappy."

In the midst of turning to leave, Abby stopped.

Eli took a step nearer. "That is not the case. I have prayed about this and *Gott* sent peace to my heart. I absolutely know what to do. I love you, Abby. I know that you believe you are barren because you didn't have a child with Abe, but I'm happy to take the risk that this may be true."

Her heart stumbling inside her, Abby rejected this, "You cannot be."

"I am," he assured her. "We cannot know that you aren't barren—*Gott* gave Sarah and Abraham a child when she was eighty. Even if we cannot have children, I want to be with you. We will care for whatever *Kinder* come our way. Perhaps we can even take in orphaned <u>Amishe</u> children. It won't matter. I cannot spend my life without you. I promise I am a reliable, trustworthy *Mann*. I loved Joanna and I lost her, but that is very different from loving you and letting you slip out of my life. Doing this would be a choice and I cannot make that choice. I love *Kinder*, but I love you more."

Abby started crying, saying angrily through her tears, "You cannot know this! You will meet some beautiful young *Maedel* who you will love."

He snorted. "Since becoming a widower, I have met—and been indifferent to—a number of *Maedels*. You know, my *Daed* had become desperate that I would never marry again. He was so relieved and grateful when I found you."

"Jobe and Rachel are lovely people," Abby said, sniffling back her tears. "They deserve grandchildren. You don't want to disappoint them."

Pulling her into his arms, Eli said, "They have grandchildren. What they really need is a son who is happy. You make me happy, Abby. I want only to kiss you the rest of my days."

"You cannot know this," she mumbled into his chest.

"I can. I have prayed and prayed about this," he told her. "Do not think I take this step without thought. I love you and I want to marry you."

Subsiding on his shoulder, Abby wept.

"Besides," Eli murmured against her temple, "you may not be barren, at all. It may have been Abe."

"Scoundrel," she said with a watery chuckle. "It's terrible to say this of a dead *Mann*."

Lifting her chin, Eli kissed her then.

"I love you, Abby Zook Eichelberger. I want to be with you, no matter what."

"You are sure?"

"I am," he said in an assured voice. "Very. Marry me. Please. If only to punish me for being a scoundrel."

Pressing the hankie he offered against her damp cheeks, Abby said, "That sounds more like you."

"I am more like me when I'm with you."

With that, Abby let him pull her into another kiss.

Thanks so much for purchasing Abigail's Admirer! If you enjoyed this book, please consider leaving a review for Abigail's Admirer, Book 3, Amish Sisters Marry Romance Series! Authors live and die by reviews and I would be very grateful if you would do me the honor of leaving one. Thanks in advance. I so appreciate it!

.

Glossary of Amish Terms:

Amische—how the Amish refer to themselves
Bickle—pickle
Bisskatz—skunk
Boppli—baby
Bopplin—babies
Bruder—brother
Buwe—boy
Daed—dad
der Suh—my son
Deerich—silly, idiotic, foolish
Dickcissels—Ohio bird
Dochder—daughter
Eldre—parents
Englischer—anyone who isn't Amish
Familye—family
Frau—wife
Geschwischder—Brothers and sister
Gmay—church group that worship together
Goedenavond—good evening
Goedemorgen—good morning
Gott—God
Grank—sick
Grossdaddi—Grandfather
Grossmammi—Grandmother
Gut—good
Guten Tag—good day
Haus—house
Heiser—houses
Kinder/Kinner—children
Liebling—sweetheart, darling, honey
Maedel—young woman
Mamm—mother

Carol Rose

Mann—man
Menner—men
Narrish—crazy
Neh—no
Schweschder—sister
Schmaert—smart
Schlang—snake
Yah—yes

About the Author

Rose Doss is an award-winning romance author. She has written thirty-one romance novels. Her books have won numerous awards, including a final in the prestigious Romance Writers of America Golden Heart Award.

A frequent speaker at writers' groups and conferences, she has taught workshops on characterization and, creating and resolving conflict. She works full time as a therapist.

Her husband and she married when she was only nineteen and he was barely twenty-one, proving that early marriage can make it, but only if you're really lucky and very persistent. They went through college and grad school together. She not only loves him still, all these years later, and she still likes him—which she says is sometimes harder. They have two funny, intelligent and highly accomplished daughters and three granddaughters, whose names all start with E like their great-grandmother, Eloise.

Rose loves writing and hopes you enjoy reading her work.

Amish Romances:

Amish By Choice (Amish Vows Romance, Prequel)
Amish Renegade(Amish Vows Romance, Bk 1)
Amish Princess(Amish Vows Romance, Bk 2)
Amish Heartbreaker(Amish Vows Romance, Bk 3)
Amish Spinster(Amish Vows Romance, Bk 4)
Amish Prodigal (Amish Vows Romance, Bk 5)
Amish Rogue(Amish Vows Romance, Bk 6)

Becca's Boy(Amish Sisters Marry Romance, Bk 1)
Dinah's Darling(Amish Sisters Marry Romance, Bk 2)
Abigail's Admirer (Amish Sisters Marry Romance, Bk 3)

www.rosedoss.com
www.twitter.com - carolrose@carolrosebooks
https://www.facebook.com/carol.rose.author